A short time later Dore stood waiting by the back steps of the school. It was getting late. Dark. She shivered a little in the cool evening air. The street-lights came on. The sound of people's voices, getting into cars, leaving, drifted back to her.

Arms closed around her. Pulled her close.

Suffocatingly close.

"Randy?" She tried to turn.

But she was held in a grip of iron. A vise.

Something flashed in front of her eyes. Claws.

She tried to pull her hands free, tried to protect herself.

The claws bore down, down.

To her face.

Also by D.E. Athkins:

Sister Dearest

point

MIRROR, MIRROR

D.E. Athkins

SCHOLASTIC INC.
New York Toronto London Auckland Sydney

ISBN 0-590-45246-0

12 11 10 9 8 7 6 5 4   3 4 5 6 7/9

Printed in the U.S.A.   01

First Scholastic printing, April 1992

Robin—so nu, cupcake?

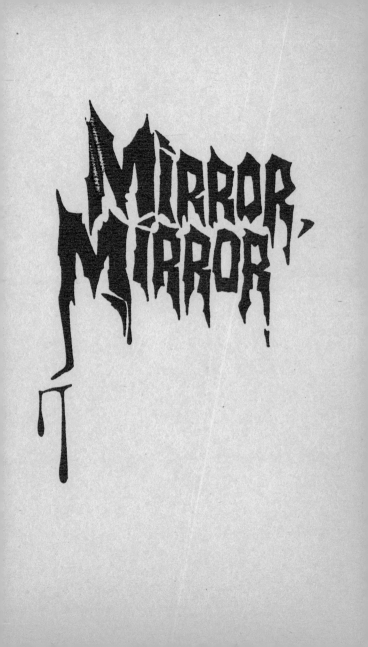

Chapter 1

"Kill, kill, KILL THEM!"

The tiger raised the blood-streaked, helmeted head high. The mob roared for more.

A girl fell forward, arms flung out, back arched, red streaming behind her.

Screams filled the air.

Then the cheerleaders at the bottom of the pyramid caught their victim, grabbed the red streamers she was holding, and flipped her in the air again so that her skirt flipped, too. The crowd rose to its feet, hot, howling, a bloodlusting mob.

It was the afterschool pep rally for the game against the Sorenson Tide that night — big, beefy Sorenson, a football team made up of big, beefy farm boys who tended to roll over smaller teams.

But not smarter teams. Not teams like the Roosevelt Tigers. They stayed low, they moved fast. And they wanted blood.

Stan Carmichael, the long, lean, lanky team mascot, was especially good at whipping the crowd to the proper frenzy. He could think up stunts like no one else. He had a way with props. A talent for the macabre.

In the stands, Gwen Forrest gave Dore Grey a poke. "He's too much!" she screamed above the noise, standing up with everyone else, clenching her fists above her head.

Dore, who had turned to look at her best friend, Gwen, pushed her sunglasses back into place and merely nodded. Her hands weren't raised above her head. She was clapping to show a sort of good faith. But she wasn't into the whole mob scene.

Besides, she'd known about the dead head. Stan had told her all about it on their date the previous weekend. His father had given him the beat-up old head of a mannequin from his department store. The football team had been more than happy to supply the helmet. Stan's big worry had been getting authentic-looking blood.

"You can send away for special blood," he'd explained seriously. "Like they use in movies. But there isn't time."

"Maybe you should send away for some anyway," she'd suggested, not at all seriously. "Lay in a supply."

"Yeah. Great idea, Dore." He'd fallen silent, then gone on. "Not ketchup. It doesn't really look right, and it doesn't hold up. Plain old makeup won't do. . . ."

"It's gruesome," shrieked Gwen as Stan paraded

up and down in front of the crowd, brandishing the head aloft.

"It's wax," said Dore. "Red melted candle wax."

"Gross," Gwen cried cheerfully.

Dore shrugged, smiling a little. It was hard to reconcile Gwen, rescuer of stray cats, rabid advocate of animal rights, hard-core vegetarian, with the girl who became a bloodthirsty maniac at sports events. She watched now as Gwen pumped her fist in the air, joining the crowd in its screaming climax. Then the rally was over.

Gwen turned to Dore with shining eyes. "We're going to kill them."

"I hope so," answered Dore. Stan was a pain when the team lost. He took it personally, as if he had somehow failed.

And of course you couldn't tell him that, ultimately, the mascot had nothing to do with it, any more than the cheerleaders, or the crowds. No, mascots didn't win, and cheerleaders didn't win, and the whole screaming crowd didn't win. Nobody on the sidelines won, thought Dore.

It was only the players who got to win.

She drifted alongside Gwen out across the parking lot to the street, half-listening to the post-rally noise making static around her. They turned toward home. Gwen talked on excitedly, letting Dore ride on "uh-huhs" at appropriate intervals. They'd been friends for a long time.

"Is Stan picking you up, or do you want me and

Carol to?" asked Gwen as they stopped in front of her house, a low ranch house that, since Gwen had shot up to just a few inches shy of six feet, made Dore want to yell "Duck!" as Gwen went in the door. Not that she would. Gwen's feelings would have been hurt.

Instead, Dore said, "Thanks, but Stan is."

"We'll save you a seat at the game, then."

"Great." Dore walked on toward her house, three blocks beyond, waving once over her shoulder without looking back.

Mrs. Bauer, their housekeeper, opened the door. "There you are," she said. "Your mother was getting worried."

"We had a pep rally today. I *told* her."

"Umm." Mrs. Bauer unfolded her arms and stepped back. "Better tell her you're here."

"Mother, I'm home!" Dore called loudly toward the back of the house, where she knew her mother was curled on her chaise lounge, reading. Ignoring Mrs. Bauer's disapproving look, she bounded up the stairs.

Her own room was in the back of the house, but, thank God, not directly above her parents'. She had huge windows, framed in swags of frothy curtains. She went over and yanked the curtains open. Her mother and Mrs. Bauer were always closing them, trying to protect the furniture. "And besides," her mother argued, "light isn't good for the skin."

But Dore loved the light. She stood back to admire the pink and gold glow of her room in the shafts of afternoon sun. No dust motes dancing in those shafts of light, though. She smiled. Mrs. Bauer saw to that.

Even though she didn't go crazy over pep rallies, Dore was pumped up a little. Edgy. Funny, it didn't usually affect her that way. She just didn't like being part of the cheering crowd. She was more used to standing above it, being cheered. Only it was her face that the crowd cheered. A face very much connected to a body — hers.

That was the way she liked her crowds. Cheering her. The winner of whatever beauty pageant she'd entered.

"I already have a cause," she always told Gwen, teasing her when Gwen tried to get Dore to march against fur or whatever. "Me."

And Gwen would shake her head and try to look disapproving and then laugh. "Bringing beauty to the world, right?" she'd shoot back.

Dore would tilt her nose and say "*Definitely. . .*"

But she meant it.

She was beautiful. She had known it for so long that in some ways, she took it for granted. Didn't even see it when she looked in the mirror. Looked only for, worked only with, the flaws that marred what other people said was her gorgeous face.

Work. That was the word. She had been working at being beautiful, more and more beautiful, ever since she could remember. Her earliest memory was of people bending over her, cooing, calling her a little angel. And her mother's pride, her cool, reserved mother's unabashed pride; and, too, the way Dore's looks had caught, momentarily, her scientifically detached father's attention.

Dore and her mother were very close now. Once Dore had understood that the praise others heaped on her own head made her mother happy, she'd been happy, too. Because it was so easy. So easy to win contests. So easy to make good grades, to step into that suit of poise that was made out of her looks.

And all she had to do was — a little work.

A little work. She dumped her books on the delicate desk and yanked open one of her drawers. She'd get suited up in her aerobics gear, then do a little workout. An extra one never hurt.

She smiled. Or even if it did, it was worth it.

Chapter 2

Personally, thought Dore, I prefer funerals.

The post-game party at Bubba Simon's house was jumping. But Stan was not.

"We should've won," he moaned.

"You *did* win," Dore pointed out for about the hundredth time.

"On a lousy field goal. What kind of win is that? We should've *crushed* them. *Mangled* them. Sucked their bones and . . ."

Dore was getting a little impatient. She didn't like these parties anyway. Stan was always there to take care of her. People were always vaguely friendly. But Stan took his role a little too seriously. He couldn't let go of it, even at the party.

Which made him a little hard to take, even if you knew him well.

And Dore knew Stan well. Had known him since they were kids. Knew him in every way there was to know him. Just about.

She sighed. "Stan. You. Won. Okay? That's what matters."

Stan shook his head. "It's how you play the game, Dore."

"No. It's not. A hundred years from now . . . five years from now, no one will remember this game. They'll just remember who won. *Winning.* That's what counts."

Mary Moran, who was cheerleading captain, and Jan Williams, her right-hand, rah-rah girl, walked by, deep in conversation. Dore studied Mary. What did Mary have that she didn't? She was cute — that was practically a legal requirement for being a cheerleader. But cute wasn't enough. Nor was perky, spirited, spunky, the whole bit. *That* would wear a person out after a while. And although she was always smiling, Dore had more than a suspicion that Mary was not a candidate for anybody's Miss Congeniality list.

Yet Mary had a great time. Mary had Corbin Durrough, arguably the best-looking, smoothest guy in the class. Mary had friends who laughed and partied, and she was always, somehow, at the center of laughing and partying.

Cute, thought Dore. *Cute. Not pretty. Definitely not beautiful.*

Just then, Mary glanced toward Dore and Stan. "Nice work, Tiger," she said, ruffling Stan's hair.

How patronizing! Stan didn't seem to realize it. He smiled sadly and said, "Thanks, Mar."

Dore looked hard at Mary. Mary didn't even notice. Now she and Jan were concentrating on giggling as they walked on by.

Probably at Stan, thought Dore glumly.

People had begun to dance. Fast, slow, so close they were standing in each other's pants, so far apart they could've been dancing alone. It didn't matter. They were having fun.

Dore wanted to dance. But she'd have to dance with Stan. Dancing with Stan was hard work. If it was a fast dance, he was a major cutup, vying for attention, the mascot of the dance floor. If it was a slow dance, he held her carefully, making little motions with his hands on her back, which made her itch. It definitely *wasn't* sexy.

She always half-expected him to pop her bra strap, like he'd done once in junior high. She'd forgiven him, because he was Stan. But she'd never forgotten.

Now Stan was explaining why winning wasn't everything. *Tell it to Miss Congeniality*, she thought. *Or the first runner-up.* But she kept quiet. If Gwen had been there, she could have talked to her. But Gwen didn't come to these post-game parties. She wasn't exactly invited.

Gwen and Carol were probably eating pizza somewhere. Half-vegetarian pizza but, still, pizza.

"You understand?" asked Stan. She looked at Stan. His sandy brown hair was tousled, his long, mobile face was tense. He had a nice mouth. She wasn't sure if he was an okay kisser or not. She didn't have enough experience. He was sweet. A little crazy, but sweet.

She sighed again. "Yes, Stan," she said.

* * *

She had a room with a view — of herself. The far wall was made of mirrors. Bottles sat on mirrors at her dressing table. Lights ringed the makeup mirror. A huge bulletin board was papered with photographs and clippings, mostly of her. Winning. Miss This. Junior Young Thing That, Little Miss Anything.

When she was famous, she was going to have one perfect portrait of herself, larger than life-sized, breathtaking, awe-inspiring, hung in some appropriate place in some appropriate mansion. Or castle.

Until then, she was, she supposed, working on her portfolio.

She crossed the room now without watching her reflection cross with her. Got undressed. Pulled on the sheer chemise and robe.

A light tap sounded at the half-open door.

"Dore? Dear?"

"Hi, Mom."

"Did you and Stan have a good time?"

"Umm," said Dore, sitting on her bed and leaning back against the headboard. Her mother came in and sat at the foot.

"It doesn't sound like you had a very good time. . . ."

Dore pulled her knees up under her chin and wrapped her arms around her legs. "I don't know."

Her mother waited. At last Dore said, "It's just that Stan's so . . ." She shrugged.

"Stan's a nice boy. Very trustworthy. He has a bright future. You may not see it now, but boys grow up later than girls."

"I guess," said Dore.

"You just have to be patient, dear. You know, nice boys aren't that easy to find."

Nice boys finish last, thought Dore.

"You're young, yet. When you get a little older, a little more out in the world, you'll meet other nice young men."

"I guess," said Dore again.

"Of course you will." Her mother got up and kissed Dore on the forehead. "Good night, dear."

" 'Night, Mother," said Dore.

After her mother left, Dore turned out her bedside light. Her pink and silver room faded into shadows. Restless, Dore got up and went over to the window.

The moon was almost full, lopsidedly round like a fat man's stomach. It was sailing belly first into the tattered clouds. As it flickered in and out, it seemed to Dore to have a reddish glow.

"The moon is just reflected light," said Dore aloud. Then she thought, that's what I am, too. Just reflected light. The reflection of my parents. I don't really know who I am at all.

"If you could be anything in the world — or *have* anything in the world — what would it be?"

Gwen examined the bottle of nail polish, frowning. "Have you ever read the ingredients in this stuff? It makes your fingernails into environmental hazards!"

"Gwennn." Dore almost frowned, then stopped herself. Frowning made wrinkles. "Call out the wrinkle squad," her mother would say whenever Dore frowned. Or whenever anything happened that made her want to frown.

"Anything in the world? That's easy — oh, here, this one's better. At least it's against animal testing."

"Yeah, well, I'm against that color. It'd look putrid on you, Gwen. . . . Here, this is the same brand, and at least it's in your color."

"Oh. Right. Good thing I brought an expert along, huh?" Gwen headed toward the cashier.

"Gwen? Are you going to answer my question?"

"If I could have anything in the world," Gwen said, "it'd be world peace."

"Figures," muttered Dore.

"What about you?" They were out in the mall now, headed toward the skating rink and the Burger Shop.

"That's just it. I don't know."

"Coke, not much ice, please," Gwen said to the boy behind the counter.

"A diet Coke," said Dore.

They took their drinks over to a table by the rink and looked down. People gyrated and spun like bits of confetti in the sunken rink below.

"I don't know what I want," said Dore.

"Rich and famous, remember?" Gwen teased. "You haven't changed your mind about that, I hope?"

Dore felt a flash of irritation. "I'm serious, Gwen."

"Sorry," said Gwen, not very contritely.

"Don't you ever feel" — Dore groped for words — "feel like everything that's happening in the whole world, all the real stuff, is happening somewhere else?"

"Like what?"

"I don't know. Things. Excitement. *Real life.*"

"You've got it all, Dore. Look at you."

"But what good does it do if all I'm doing is going out with Stan, and bringing home good grades, and making my parents say, 'Good girl, Dore'?"

Gwen slurped her Coke noisily, and Dore winced. It was useless to try to explain anything to Gwen. Gwen the literal-minded. Gwen the princess of practical. How could Gwen ever understand how maddening it was to be so — so *understood* by her proud, protective parents? How could Gwen, who didn't date, ever understand that dating Stan wasn't the outer limits of anyone's ambition? How could Gwen understand that Dore could want more, even if she wasn't sure what more was?

"You just need a change," suggested Gwen. "Maybe it's time you got involved in a good cause. . . ."

"No. No marches, no campaigns, no causes."

Gwen shrugged, and Dore sighed and looked

down at the confetti-people. Suddenly her eyes narrowed.

Flashing among the skaters was a girl dressed in red, with burning red hair streaming out behind her. She danced over the ice like a flame.

"Who's that?" asked Dore.

Gwen looked down, too. "Who?"

"In the red."

They both watched. The girl was in a unitard, with a red-and-yellow muffler wrapped around her throat. Her hair seemed to have its own life, snaking and flying in thick ropes and curls around her face.

"Wow," said Gwen.

Finishing a spin, the girl stopped. She looked around, as if she were lost. No, not as if she were lost. Something about the way she raised her chin, nose high, made it seem as if she were testing the air for a scent.

As if, thought Dore, she were hunting.

Suddenly, the girl's head turned. It was a startling motion, the quick turn of the head atop the poised and perfect and motionless body.

"Like in *The Exorcist,* wow," murmured Gwen.

The girl's eyes slid over the ringside crowd, slid over Gwen, slid on to Dore. And stopped.

Dore felt the rush of her heart in her chest, hot. Burning.

She pushed back from the table. "I'm . . . let's go. It's cold in here."

"Cold," said Gwen, rising obediently.

"Cold," snapped Dore. "I'm freezing. To death."

Chapter 3

"There she goes . . ." Stan, singing off-key and *loud*, pretending to be old Bert Parks himself. Everyone turned around to look, and Dore raised her chin, ignoring them. Some things at Roosevelt High never changed, even when you were a senior.

"Hey, beautiful." Stan put his hand on the back of her neck. It was the way they always walked together. But this time she pulled away.

"Don't," she said and stopped, oblivious now to the other students around her. The warning bell for class sounded.

"Don't what?" asked Stan.

"Don't call me beautiful, okay?" she snapped.

It was out of character for her to snap — so out of character for her even to have a strong opinion — that Stan was disconcerted. He just stood there.

He looked so stunned, so — if such a thing were possible in someone so self-absorbed — hurt, that she almost apologized. After all, they'd been together for years. He was a cute guy. . . .

But cute is not enough, said a voice in her head.

The voice startled her. She stopped herself from looking wildly around. Get a grip, Dore, she admonished herself. She took a deep breath.

Stan looked expectant. Now a maddening little grin hovered around his mouth.

And she pressed her mouth firmly closed and didn't apologize. Instead, she started walking again — away from Stan.

The word repeated in her head as she left: beautiful, beautiful, beautiful.

Along with an echo in a new voice: so what, so what, so what?

After dinner that night, she went up to her room and pulled on her workout outfit. She began to stretch, pushing, making herself hurt. She watched herself as she worked, turning, twisting, flexing. She watched the ripple of muscle, the glisten of sweat, the expressions on her face.

It was kind of a turn-on, she had to admit. She wondered what it would be like to be working out with a guy like this.

Get a grip, she told herself for the second time that day. You want some gorgeous guy to see you sweat?

Sweetie, said the voice, you want to make *him* sweat.

Dore froze right in the middle of one of the stomach thrusts.

"What?" she said aloud and turned around, just to make sure. Just to make sure she was alone in the room.

She was. If you didn't count the mirrors and the photographs.

What is *wrong* with me? she thought, and plunged back into her workout twice as hard as before.

When the phone rang, she knew it was Stan. Without missing a beat, she reached over and turned the ringer off, then bent from the waist, palms on the floor between her outstretched legs, pushing, pushing.

Somewhere in the house, the phone kept ringing.

Her mother's voice came coolly up the stairs.

"Telephone, Dore. Stan."

Dore didn't jump up. She didn't call back, "Just a minute, thank you." She didn't do any of the things she normally would have done. She envisioned her mother, waiting sedately at the bottom of the stairs. She envisioned Stan, jittering on the other end of the phone.

If your mother likes Stan so much, let her talk to him. . . .

Dore gasped, then called quickly, "Tell him I'll call him back."

"I'm sorry, dear. I didn't quite hear you."

And Dore heard herself say, in perfect Queen B style, "I SAID, tell him I'll call him back."

She bent forward, her chest almost on the ground between her hands, chin almost resting on the carpet. She stared into the mirror, stared into her eyes.

After a minute, she sensed that her mother had gotten the message.

She smiled at herself in the mirror.

Mrs. Bauer was just pouring the coffee when Dore came down to breakfast the next day. She stopped to look at her parents for a moment: Her mother, with her sleek gold-and-silver hair pulled back into a perfect French twist, sitting carefully with her back to the sun, which filtered in through the sheer curtains, toying with her food; her father, thin, upright, motionless, only his eyes behind his half-glasses moving across the pages of his eternal horticultural journals.

"Morning, Miss Dorothy," said Mrs. Bauer, and both of Dore's parents looked up.

"Good morning, Mrs. Bauer," said Dore.

"Can I get you anything?"

"No — I'll get it myself. Thanks."

She felt her mother's eyes on her, studying her as she helped herself to toast and coffee from the sideboard. She sighed inwardly, then turned.

Her father had looked up, too, his deceptively mild gaze traveling back and forth between Dore and her mother. So she smiled at both of them, a big, just-won-the-pageant smile. Reassured, her father returned to his reading.

But her mother kept watching her as if she were puzzled. Not frowning, of course. No wrinkle squad for her. But, then, thought Dore suddenly, smiling gave you wrinkles, too. Didn't it?

"Dore? Dear?" her mother said.

"Hmm?" Dore slid into her usual place at the long, gleaming mahogany table. She glanced down at her reflection in the table's mirrored surface. Ugh — not her best angle. She set her plate down quickly.

She remembered the day her mother had had the table delivered. Her father had wandered through as her mother was ordering the increasingly irritated deliverymen to move it into a fractionally different place for about the hundredth time.

"Mahogany," he'd commented in his typical telegraph style. "Tropical forests. Environmentally destructive."

But her mother had been ready. "Plantation mahogany, Cal."

Typically, her father had drifted back out to his greenhouses without further comment.

Dore smiled at her reflection, then looked up and smiled again at her mother. "What is it?"

Mrs. Grey relaxed. "Nothing. You know, maybe you've been working too hard. Maybe we should do a little shopping this afternoon. Get you some really special clothes. After all, this is your senior year."

"That'd be great, Mom," said Dore.

She suddenly felt reassured. What had been wrong with her? Oh, well, whatever it was, it was nothing she couldn't handle. Nothing, probably, that spending a little green, wearing out a little plastic, wouldn't help.

She would remember thinking that later on. And smile — at first — at just how wrong she had been.

Going up the steps of Eleanor Roosevelt High that morning, she saw the back of Stan's bomber jacket and headed toward it, already seeing herself smiling ruefully, laying her hand on his arm, apologizing with a little silly-me laugh.

But someone was already standing by Stan, smiling, hand on his sleeve.

Dore hesitated only an instant. Years of walking up and down ramps and aisles had taught her how to recover from a stumble, after all. She even used the fractional pause to take it all in: how elegantly poised the girl was, how the color of her hair seemed to change in the sun from blazing red to spinning gold, how little glints like fire came off the earrings in her ears, chains at her throat, bracelets on her wrist. The girl gave off heat.

Dore saw it all in an instant and kept walking up the stairs, head high, not looking down. She was so good at it that no one possibly could have noticed her pause and size up the girl on Stan's arm.

Except that as Dore had hesitated for that one fleeting moment, she'd met the girl's glinting green eyes. And recognized her. The girl from the skating rink.

And Dore could have sworn that the girl knew exactly what Dore was thinking.

"Hello, Stan," said Dore. She cradled her elbows in her hands and waited.

He jumped, gulped, and then stammered, "D-dore!"

"I know," said Dore kindly. "It's not every day I come to school."

She waited again, and Stan seemed finally to regain control of his speech. "Yeah. Dore — this is Lucinda. She's new."

Dore held out her hand, along with the smile she usually used for the second runner-up. "Hello, Lucinda. Welcome to Ellie Roosevelt."

Lucinda kept her hand on Stan's arm just a moment longer, her own smile wider, more amused somehow. She was, Dore noted, wearing burning red lipstick that should have looked wrong, especially on those pouty, bad girl lips. But, somehow, she pulled it off. And, suddenly, Dore, who knew she was a thousand times more gorgeous than this Lucinda, felt plain. Sexless. Boring.

She hated it.

Then Lucinda was taking Dore's hand in her own and turning it over. "Call me Luci," she said. "With an i." She bent over Dore's palm.

"What are you doing?" asked Dore, resisting the urge to snatch her hand back as if it had touched a hot oven.

"Looking at your future. Looking at your fortune."

One of those, thought Dore. Aloud she said flatly, "Oh . . . how interesting. What do you see?"

"A tall, *built* guy," said Luci. She looked out of the corner of her eye at Stan, and he turned red.

The first bell rang, and the general shift up the stairs and into the school began. Luci dropped Dore's hand, and Dore had to resist the urge to rub it against her skirt, like some little kid.

Stan stood there. Torn, Dore thought, between loyalty and another big l-word. She saved him the trouble.

"See you," she said and turned away. But not before she saw the quick look of relief in Stan's eyes. And the little smile curling the edge of Luci's lips.

She didn't see Luci or Stan for the rest of the day.

Chapter 4

She said, as casually as possible, "Have you seen Stan?"

Gwen, who was pulling various items wrapped in waxed paper out of a brown paper bag, shook her head. "Why? Is he wearing something weird?"

"Sure — a fur coat . . . just kidding," Dore added quickly.

Gwen grinned, shaking her head again as Dore scanned the lunchroom. It was packed, the volume on high. But no Stan. And no Luci, either.

Which led Dore to conclude that they were missing the action together. Or making some of their own.

"Dore? Is anything the matter? With you and Stan?"

"Why?" shot back Dore. "Waiting for your big chance?"

Gwen froze, her sprout-and-whatever sandwich halfway to her mouth.

"Just *kidding*," said Dore. "Look. Here comes

Carol." She didn't notice the dull blush that had spread up Gwen's neck and cheeks.

"Pop test in Dillard the Dullard's history class," announced Carol, plopping her tray down and putting a fat history book next to it. "Pass the word."

Gwen groaned. "Great. He probably just didn't want to teach us anything today."

"When has he ever taught us anything?" cracked Carol. "Except to despise and *de*test history?"

"You liked it to begin with?" inquired Dore. They all cracked up then.

"One for you, Dore!" Carol's pointed, puckish face looked even more impish, if possible. If Gwen was the epitome of serious, the queen of causes, Carol was a joker, a practical joker in the first degree, and a wild card. In some ways, she was like Stan. But where Stan wanted all the world to admire his special effects, Carol would pull her jokes anywhere, anytime. Her bizarre sense of humor had gotten her in trouble more than once, but it had never stopped her. She was the sort of person who laughed riotously through horror movies. She rated them according to the amount of blood spilled. "Now that," she would observe, "was a three-bucket movie."

"Listen, someone should put Dillard out of his misery," said Carol. "And ours."

"Any ideas, Carol?" prompted Gwen.

"It'll come to me," said Carol. She bent her gaze on her history book. "It'll come to me."

"Mind if I join you?"

They looked up. It was Luci.

For a moment they were all still. Gwen looked almost apprehensive. Carol's narrow blue eyes gleamed with curiosity. Dore kept her own face blank.

Luci kept smiling easily. "Sure," said Carol at last. "Sit away."

"Fascinating food," said Luci as she settled her tray next to Carol's.

"Isn't it?" asked Carol.

"I'm Lucinda; everyone calls me Luci."

"I'm Carol, this is Gwen, and this is — "

"We've met," Dore interrupted. "Luci's a fortune-teller. You should get her to tell your fortune."

"Quick," said Carol. "Will I pass the history test today? Or will Dillard maybe take a quick trip down the stairs — head first, saving my butt?"

Luci smiled. "Anything can happen."

"You're new here?" asked Gwen. She gave Dore a look that said, "Why didn't you tell me about her?"

"Umm," said Luci. "Interesting school. Who are those people over there?"

Carol turned. "The jocks, the cheerleaders . . . the usual."

"I see."

Dore's eyes glanced at the table involuntarily, a table that most of the cafeteria was also watching outright or covertly. Corbin was there. He still had a tan, although the summer was long gone. He wore his dark hair a little long. She knew, although she couldn't see from where she sat, that his eyes were sea-green. And she *could* see, quite clearly, that he had a great bod.

"I don't see Stan," observed Luci.

"He's working on a pep-rally project. He's the mascot," said Dore. *As if you didn't know.*

"Of course. I knew. Very creative," said Luci.

"Where're you from?" asked Carol.

Luci shrugged. "No place interesting. Unless you like hot weather."

"Some — " Carol paused significantly, to make sure everyone got it — "some like it hot."

Gwen said, "The worst, Carol."

"I like it here," Luci went on.

"Definitely you're new. This school is the pits. . . ."

"What school isn't?" said Luci.

"So what's to like?"

"The people, Carol. Lots of potential here."

"And definitely you're an optimist," answered Carol.

Gwen pulled out an apple (an organic one, if I know Gwen, thought Dore) and took a bite. Luci watched her, amused.

Noticing Luci's scrutiny, Gwen flushed a little, then asked politely, "Want some?"

"N-no. Thank you. Although I'm very partial to apples." Luci suddenly threw back her head and laughed. It was a golden, seductive sound, and Carol and Gwen, for no reason at all, joined in.

Dore watched.

"Listen," said Luci, her face merry and glowing.

"What are you guys doing after school?"

"Carol and I were going to study. . . . You want to join us?" asked Gwen.

"I'd love it," said Luci. "What about you, Dore?"

"No," said Dore. "Thanks, anyway."

She was angry — angry at Gwen and Carol for being so easily taken in, angry at this new girl, who could just waltz up and be included, angry at Stan's apparent easy defection. Luci was a, was a . . . Dore searched her mind for a suitable word. Nothing current came to mind, but what was that old-fashioned word she'd heard her mother use? Vamp . . . Yes. That was it. Vamp. It sounded just right.

Standing up, Dore said coolly, "See you guys later."

Dore could feel their eyes on her back: Carol's curious, Gwen's confused, Luci's — amused? Dore clenched her teeth and slowed down and smiled extravagantly at Mary Moran as she passed the cheerleaders' table. Mary was leaning back, her hand on Corbin's arm. She let her eyes slide down Dore, then up again to meet Dore's eyes. Then she smiled back, a tiny, contemptuous smile. Who are you? the smile asked smugly.

Then Mary looked at Corbin, leaned forward, and said something to the table at large. Several more pairs of eyes looked her way, followed by a burst of laughter.

Dore was stunned. And then she was very, very angry. Murderously angry. She met Mary's eyes again, saw Mary's triumphant expression. And she felt the murderous rage fill her eyes; she felt as if she were on fire.

She looked hard at Mary. The laughter died down as the two girls looked at each other.

Then Dore smiled.

Only it wasn't really a smile.

She walked on by. She left a little silence in her wake. A silence quickly swallowed by the lunchroom roar.

When she got to her locker, she looked down. Her hands were clenched into fists, clenched so tightly that her nails had dug little, faintly bloodied half-moons in her palms.

"Too bad it's my blood," she thought, looking down. "Too bad it isn't Mary Moran's." She smiled her not-real smile again. And said aloud, "Next time, it will be."

Chapter 5

Two people in the mirror: Dore and Gwen. Gwen was sitting with her back to the mirror, idly stroking one of Dore's stuffed animals, a mink-plush Gund bear.

"You know," she said, "if they can make these stuffed animals so nice and soft, what's the point of fur coats, anyway?"

"What, are you trying to skin my stuffed animals now?" said Dore. She smiled at Gwen to show she was kidding.

Gwen smiled back. Not a bad smile, thought Dore. Too bad she is such a way serious person. Never get anywhere like that . . .

She pushed the thought away. She and Gwen were old friends. Best friends, she told herself firmly. Gwen was just Gwen, that's all. No big deal.

Resting her chin on the bear's head, Gwen asked, "Are you going to the party this weekend? The one at Megan Holland's?"

"Even if I were speaking to Stan, which I am not . . ."

"But — "

"Gwen, Stan acted like some drooling dog around Luci. With me standing there."

"But he called. He said it was a misunderstanding."

"Oh, I understood. Perfectly."

"Well, it wasn't Luci's fault. . . ."

"We're getting off the subject. Am I going to Megan's party this Saturday? I don't think so. You know my parents, Gwen. Only the right parties, with the right people — like Bubba's boring parties, with Stan."

"They'd let you go if you asked."

"If I begged, you mean. And if I don't tell them that Megan's parents are out of town. And if I don't tell them that I'm not going with Stan. . . ."

"Mmm." Gwen flopped back on the bed and looked up at the ceiling. "I wish I could go."

"So go."

"I couldn't do that! By myself."

"Yeah . . ." Dore looked back down at the magazine she'd been reading.

Gwen kept talking. Background noise. Dore barely even noticed when she stopped.

"Dore?"

Dore turned the page.

"Dore? What do you think?"

"About what?"

"We could go together."

Dore looked at Gwen in surprise. "How?"

"You could sleep over at my house."

"Gwen! You mean, like, *lie* to my parents? *You* are actually suggesting that I lie?"

"Not lie," said Gwen. "You just don't have to tell them. And my parents will be cool about it, especially if we're going together."

"This is not like you, Gwen. Definitely it is not like you." Dore paused and looked at the girl she thought she knew so well. "But, yes, let's do it."

Gwen gave a happy bounce. "This'll be great!"

"Yeah, it will." But Dore had a feeling she and Gwen weren't talking about the same thing.

Opening the door of Gwen's parents' reliable, boring, well-kept old car, Dore surveyed the neighborhood. Cars were parked on the ragged curbs up and down both sides of the street. Megan didn't live in the best neighborhood. It was middle class on the downside. No way a party like this would pass unnoticed anywhere else.

It was already late. And everyone was pumped, you could tell. The shadows of people merged and whispered in the darkness, out by the cars, and in the deeper dark under the trees. As Dore walked toward the Hollands' house with Gwen, she could hear the music, feel it. The ground beneath her feet seemed to have a crazy pulse all its own.

The front door of the brick house was slightly ajar. Dore put her hand on it to push it open and felt the pulse there, too. It gave her a rush.

"Feel," she said, turning to Gwen.

"What?" said Gwen loudly.

"Feel."

Gwen shook her head, pretending to put her hands over her ears. And then a voice spoke so closely, so softly, in Dore's ear that she almost thought it was the voice inside her head again: "She wouldn't feel a thing."

Dore turned her head slightly, slowly. It was Luci, smiling.

"Welcome," said Luci. She held out two cups. After a slight hesitation, Gwen took hers. "THANK YOU," she yelled.

"JUST PUNCH," said Luci back. She watched as Gwen took a small sip.

Gwen seemed surprised. "IT'S GOOD."

"No, thanks," said Dore.

"Wise choice." Luci put her free hand on the door and pushed it open. They plunged into the party.

The noise poured over them, swallowing them and all thought. Luci threaded her way through the crowd of pumping bodies, not all of them moving to the music, beneath the somehow obscene strings of gyrating jalapeño pepper lights that crisscrossed the ceiling. Gwen followed obediently in her wake, tilting the cup back for a deeper drink.

Dore pressed herself against the wall and watched them disappear into the darkness. Guess what, Gwen, she thought. You're not in Kansas anymore.

And neither are you, Dorothy. For one dry-mouthed minute, she stayed there. Listening to her own internal voice. The one that said, you don't belong here. Go home. You don't even know how to act. You should be here with Stan. What if Stan finds out? What if your parents . . .

Then a tall, dark figure slid down the wall and stopped next to her. She looked up, heart pounding. Tom Connors. Not a nice boy. Depending, of course, on what you meant by nice.

"It's me," he said confidently, as if he were taking up the middle of a conversation.

She took a deep breath and said the first thing that came into her head. "You're back," she answered. From somewhere a laugh bubbled up. Pretty stupid, Dorothy, she thought. But she kept the smile on her face, and leaned forward just a little.

"Gone," he said. "What I am is gone. Gone-gone."

"The punch," suggested Dore.

"Think of it as fruit. Good f'you."

"I think I'd like to dance," said Dore. "Are you up for it?"

"I'll get up for it," he said, leaning closer.

Dore stepped away from the wall, catching his arm firmly in her hands, and pulled him into the cauldron of bodies and sound.

I did it, she thought. It was so easy. The pulse of the music burned through her . . . and it was so easy, too, to dance right on the edge of it all.

She'd never danced like this with Stan.

After that, the night turned into streamers of movement and color and heat. She danced a long time with Tom, segueing effortlessly from one beat to the next, one song to another. Then, another guy, one of the basketball players named Skip, suddenly materialized and pulled her into a play, and started a whole set of new moves.

Spinning out at the end of Skip's fingertips, she smiled at Tom and he smiled back, his teeth white in the darkness. "Baby, baby," he said hoarsely and melted back into the crowd, in the direction of the punch.

After Skip, another guy, and then another, until at last she was all used up, too tired to go on. She fell against her partner — Randy — and he patted her shoulder.

"Something to drink?"

"Please," she said. She edged toward the arm of a sofa, which was largely occupied by an oblivious horizontal couple — or maybe it was three people, or four, hard to see in the darkness — and took a seat on the end by their feet. Somewhere nearby a girl shrieked, then burst into hiccuping laughter. The music smoothed out somewhat, and couples began to lean into one another.

She saw Randy pushing back through the clutch, two drinks held aloft. Over his shoulder she saw a flash of red hair, a red that was almost black in the dark.

Then Randy stopped in front of her, grinning, and handed her the cup. She took a sip and wrinkled her nose. "What's in this stuff — gasoline?"

He guffawed loudly, and shoved his arm hard against the beefy guy who stopped beside him. And then there was Luci.

"Having fun, Dore?" she asked.

Dore smiled noncommittally, and put down her drink. "Are you?" she said.

"What's the matter?" said Luci softly. "Afraid to be yourself? Afraid to have fun?"

For an outraged moment, Dore thought she hadn't heard right. "You've got to be kidding," she said stiffly.

"Oh, no. No." Luci slipped a hand beneath each boy's elbow. "It's a great party, isn't it?"

"Gettin' better all the time," said Randy.

The music went up another notch. "Uh-oh," said the beefy guy. "This is gonna crank the neighbors. We'll be doing the policeman's ball, if someone isn't careful."

"Maybe it's time to go," said Luci. "Dore?"

Something nibbled at the edge of Dore's consciousness.

She looked at Luci's laughing face. She suddenly saw Mary Moran, sitting at the cafeteria table, laughing, laughing.

Luci didn't seriously think she was going to fall for that line about being scared to enjoy herself. Did she?

Then, suddenly, Tom was back, swaying a little. Laughing a little.

Luci threw back her head and laughed some

more. It was a sound as cool as water on your skin on a hot day. The sound of someone who loved to take life on.

It wasn't that Luci was bad, thought Dore. It's just that her own pleasure came first.

And why shouldn't it? she thought. Who else was going to put you first?

Luci had stopped laughing.

Dore looked directly at her. She said, speaking as softly as Luci had spoken to her, "What are you saying, Luci?"

Watching Dore, Luci took a sip from the cup she was holding. "Want some?" she asked.

Hardly noticing what she did, Dore took the cup. "What *are* you saying, Luci?"

"You try so hard to be nice," said Luci. "Why? Nice is what people are when they can't be anything else. And what good does it do?"

Concentrating on Luci, feeling something indefinable stir in her veins, a faint thrum of excitement, of *possibilities*, Dore took a sip from the cup. The party seemed to be a vast hurricane, with them in the center.

The drink burned her lips and throat, but she hardly noticed. She handed the cup back to Luci, suddenly seeing through new eyes, suddenly understanding — what? She wasn't exactly sure. Yet.

"Nice girls finish last? Is that what you're trying to say, Luci?"

Luci gave a little gurgle of laughter. "When they finish at all."

"Dance?" Tom said. And the party closed over their heads once more. The intensity of the dancing. The ragged heat of bodies. The hallucinatory lights. The mind-possessing music.

"No," said Dore. "No." She stood up and leaned close to Tom. "I have a better idea. Come on."

Tom followed her without resisting as she pulled him out of the darkened room. On the way out, she caught sight of Gwen pressed against a wall, swaying slightly. Gwen didn't look so good, thought Dore. Not so good at all.

For a moment she hesitated. Then, with new clarity, she saw the night ahead if she went over to Gwen. It wouldn't be any fun driving home with her. She might even get arrested for drunk driving. Or Dore would have to drive. And Gwen would be very, very sick. And her parents would want to know why. And . . .

"C'mon," she said to Tom.

The street outside seemed very still and dark, like something kept at bay by the scream and pump of the music.

"Where's your car?"

Without answering, Tom took the lead. The car was low and silver and sleek, cantilevered up on the sidewalk of the house across the street.

She opened the door without waiting, leaned across and pushed the driver's door open. She saw his smile in the dark.

"I'd just love a ride home," she said. "But not straight home . . ."

He laughed softly and turned the key. The car roared instantly to life. He grabbed her hand and put it under his as he shifted the gears, bucking them free, turning up on the lawn and spinning back down across the sidewalk into the street.

The lights of the house came on as they straightened out and headed for the corner.

She looked back as they rounded it. The blue flash of lights from approaching cop cars.

Tom looked in his rearview mirror and grinned.

"Party's over," he said.

She took her hand off his and touched his knee, lightly.

"Maybe," she said.

Chapter 6

"Dore?"

Dore groaned. Where was she?

Megan Holland's party . . . where were her clothes?

She opened her eyes. Closed them again.

Her room. Her mother's voice.

But where were her clothes? And her night-gown . . .

Then she remembered. Last night. Her lips curved upward in a sleepy smile.

"Dear?"

"Hmmm."

"A — friend is here to see you."

"Hmmm. Later, Mom, okay?"

"Is that any way to treat a — friend?"

Luci.

Dore opened her eyes slowly. But she was in time to see her mother's frown. And the way Luci insinuated herself between Dore's mother and the doorframe, until she was inside the room.

Sitting up, Dore made a grab at the sheets just in time.

"Hope you're feeling better," said Luci, coming in and sitting down at the foot of Dore's bed. She smiled, revealing her small, white teeth.

"Better . . . sure."

"Well," said her mother from the doorway. "Don't visit too long, girls. I don't want you to have a relapse, Dore."

"No, Mom," said Dore.

Luci asked, "Could you close the door behind you?"

"Dore," said her mother, her face tight with disapproval.

Dore almost laughed. God, Luci had nerve.

"Thanks, Mom . . . okay?" Dore held her breath. They all waited.

Finally her mother closed the door.

"Whew," said Luci. She held out her hand. On it was a package wrapped in red paper. "Happy birthday."

"It's not my birthday!"

"Sure it is. The beginning of the first day of the rest of your life, right?"

Dore plucked at the ribbon. "What is it?"

"Something someone once gave to me. It's very old. And very, very valuable."

"Then, why — oh!" Folded back, the wrapping revealed a heavy and old-fashioned looking mirror inside an ornate silver frame.

Dore lifted it out of the tissue, feeling its heavy warmth. She turned it over. The back was decorated with the tiny figures of animals — unlike any animals Dore had ever seen.

She looked up to find Luci watching her. "Pre-flood types," said Luci cryptically. "You like?"

"It's beautiful. But I can't . . ."

"Sure you can. Look."

Luci came and sat by Dore, and turned the mirror back over. Although it was not large, it gave back the reflection of both their faces.

It also gave back a kind of gleam. Dore's lips parted as she stared at herself.

"You will keep it?" asked Luci, standing up. "I want you to have it. It's — special."

Dore nodded slowly. Her reflection nodded, too — beautifully. Gracefully.

Luci stood up. "We'll talk about last night another time. Yes?"

The reflection in the mirror ran its tongue over its lips and said, "Yes."

"Good." From the threshold of the room, Luci looked back. "Mirror, mirror on the wall, who's the fairest of them all, Dore?"

Dore didn't answer.

Luci smiled. "You're it," she said.

And left.

The world was made of silver glass. She stepped into a hall of mirrors and saw herself, as beautiful as Cinderella. She had never been so perfect, so beautiful. But as she walked toward her reflection, the mirrors began to dissolve. She walked straight into herself.

Now the silver was pouring down on her in molten webs.

"You shouldn't have," said a mournful voice.

Dore turned. "Gwen!"

The creature that looked like Gwen but wasn't, smiled. "What a bad girl," it hissed.

And Dore's dress began to dissolve wherever the silver touched it. Hissing . . .

Dore turned wildly, running back out of the mirror — only to meet herself in a thousand other mirrors.

But Dore was no longer beautiful. Everywhere the silver had touched her had turned to naked, rotting flesh. Like the wicked witch in *The Wizard of Oz* she was . . .

Melting. . . .

"No!" Somehow Dore was out of her bed. Her sleep-glazed eyes met her own image in the mirrors that lined her wall. Terrified, she picked up the first thing that came to hand.

She hurled it at the mirrors.

A horrible rending sound, like the screams of thousands of tiny dying animals, made her fall to her knees atop the clothes she had dropped on the floor the night before, her hands pressed to her ears.

"Stop it!" she screamed. "Stop it!"

"Dore!" Her mother's voice.

"No! No!"

"Dore, stop."

Dore looked up. One section of her mirrored wall was webbed with cracks. On the floor below lay the mirror that Luci had given her.

"Oh, no," gasped Dore. She lunged forward and snatched up the mirror.

It was unharmed. She turned it over and saw her face, her eyes wild and strange in the early morning light.

Her mother was bending over her. Hastily Dore struggled to her feet, turning the mirror away from her mother.

"A-a nightmare, Mom. Too much sleep, maybe."

"Maybe you shouldn't go to school today," said her mother.

Sanity was returning. The long Sunday spent in bed, sleeping and waking and telling her mother she felt too bad to talk on the phone to Gwen. Luci's visit. The phone call, too, from Randy. She was almost surprised he called, after she'd gone off with Tom like that at the party. But Tom was just a one-night entertainment, a girl toy. Everyone knew that. She hadn't talked to Randy yet. She'd see him at school today. . . .

She got to her feet and laid down the mirror carefully on her bedside table. "I rested all day yesterday, Mother. I'm fine."

"But Dore. Dear."

"It was just this dream. Can we fix the mirror?"

"Of course, dear. What about some coffee?"

"Coffee. Yes. Coffee would be nice."

After her mother left, Dore picked up the mirror. As she raised it up, she became aware of a stinging sensation in her finger. Ugh. She'd cut herself. She didn't remember doing that.

She realized it must have been when she picked up the mirror. How else would it have gotten those three red drops of blood smeared across it?

Her face looked back out from behind the smears at her, as if her reflection peered out from behind bloody prison bars.

"Ugh," said Dore, groping for a tissue to wipe the red smears off the mirror. "Definitely *not* my best color. . . ."

There. Clean and shiny and, well, not new, but as good as. She started to put the mirror down again, then stopped. It was too valuable to just leave out. She looked around the room, then went over to the low bookcase and carefully slid the mirror down behind the books on the top shelf.

"There," she said aloud, and began to get ready for school.

"I need to talk to you. Now."

Dore almost yawned. Gwen was *so* predictable. Why hadn't she ever noticed before? "Please, Gwen. It's dawn."

"It's almost lunch."

"I don't feel so good."

"Well, you shouldn't," said Gwen.

"Okay," said Dore, stifling another yawn. "Go on.

Let me have it, Gwen." She stepped back just a little, involuntarily. Gwen looked so — so angry. Not like Gwen at all. Like someone else. Suddenly the dream came back to her . . . Gwen!

Dore gave a little gasp, but Gwen didn't notice. "Dore, why didn't you answer my phone calls? Where did you *go* Saturday night?"

"Out," Dore managed to say. But she kept seeing the dream-Gwen. The nightmare Gwen . . . what did it mean?

"Doree."

"Are you going to ask me what I did?"

"Dore! Are you listening to me? You'd better be!"

Dore pulled herself together and focused on Gwen. Tears. Gwen never cried!

"Gwen. We went to the party together. But we did not say we'd stay joined at the hip. I got a ride home with a guy."

"To your house. You were supposed to sleep over at mine."

"Don't worry. My mom didn't ask any questions. I told her I wasn't feeling well." Dore started edging down the hall.

"I'm lucky I wasn't killed," said Gwen hotly. "The cops came, did you know that? I got — sick. And I almost got arrested. What if my parents found out?"

"Did anybody get arrested?"

"N-no."

"Well, there," said Dore. "What's the problem?"

"The problem is, I thought we were friends." She paused.

"Oh," said Dore. Finally. She watched Gwen's pale face grow flushed.

"Dore?"

"I'm here . . . where else would I be?"

"Dore, we are friends, aren't we?"

"I should be insulted, right? I mean, how long have we been friends? And you ask me now if we are."

Now it was her turn to wait. Slowly, Gwen nodded.

Wimp, thought Dore.

"It turned out okay, didn't it?" Dore pressed her advantage. "And, look, if you got an eye for a guy, I wouldn't want to hold you back. You wouldn't want me to."

Gwen nodded, a little less uncertainly.

"Good. Listen . . ."

"Hey, hey."

"Randy." He leaned against her, just a little, just enough to let her know how he felt.

Which was good.

She smiled. She leaned back a little, straightening her shoulders.

"I called you," he said.

"I was — worn out," Dore answered.

Gwen frowned. The expression in her eyes was not reassuring. "Dore?"

"Um-hmm."

"Uh, do you want to . . ."

"You go on, Gwen," said Dore. "Don't let me keep you."

Gwen frowned heavily. Then she said, "Oh! Oh, okay. See you later, Dore."

Not if I see you first, said the little voice inside Dore's head. Only it wasn't a strange voice after all. She'd been mistaken. It was her voice. It was Dore's own voice.

Chapter 7

"Nice," said Dore as the doorman stepped back to let them pass, touching the brim of his cap.

"I thought you'd approve," answered Luci, leading the way through the marble-floored lobby paneled from floor to ceiling with mirrors. Dore watched the two of them as Luci led the way into the mahogany-paneled elevators.

"The top," Luci said to the elevator operator.

Dore had the momentarily giddy sensation of falling as the elevator shot upward. Then the doors were opening, and they were walking down a long, thickly carpeted hall. Luci unlocked the door at the end and went in, dropping her book bag carelessly on a side table in the foyer.

"*Nice* view." Dore stopped in the foyer for a moment, staring across the endless stretch of parquet floor to the wall of windows at the far end of the living room.

Luci didn't even look. She kicked off her shoes

and disappeared through a door to one side of the room. "I'll be with you in a minute," she called back to Dore. "Make yourself at home."

Dore slowly moved forward, her eyes still on the panorama below her, flushed fiery red by the setting sun. After putting her books down on a delicate secretary set in a niche at one side of the windows, she drifted around the room. Everything was pale, pale with the untouched feeling of newness. She ran her hands over a silver dish heaped with red apples, the one bright splash of color in the room.

A bowl of darker apples filled a painting to one side of the room. No photographs or personal items graced the pale surfaces of tables; a vase filled with large white feathers, like the feathers from an enormous swan's wing, stood on the table behind the couch.

This room, thought Dore, is as silent as a tomb. She shuddered involuntarily, and hastily sank into a deep, silk-brocade chair.

A moment later, Luci reappeared carrying two champagne flutes and a little crystal dish set in ice. Behind her, a wooden-faced man followed, holding a tray containing a wine bucket filled with ice chilling a bottle of champagne, two mother-of-pearl spoons, and what looked like white toast with the crusts cut off.

"What's this?"

The wooden-faced man settled the tray carefully on the coffee table, then opened the champagne and filled the flutes. "That'll be all," said Luci, and Dore was reminded of how she had coolly dismissed her mother.

When the wooden-faced man had gone, Luci handed one flute to Dore, holding the other aloft by the stem between her fingertips.

"Champagne and caviar, to answer your question. We're celebrating."

"What are we celebrating? Where are your parents?"

"Taste it."

Dore took a hesitant sip and wrinkled her nose a little. "It doesn't taste like champagne."

Luci smiled. "I'll bet you're used to that pink stuff — the drink of beauty pageants and weddings, right?"

"Well . . ." said Dore noncommittally.

Luci spooned caviar onto a triangle of toast and passed it to Dore. Dore tasted the caviar and frowned. She took a healthy swallow of champagne to wash it down.

"Ugh. *That's* caviar?"

Luci devoured a wedge of toast, licking her lips with catlike satisfaction.

"That's caviar. . . . If you could see the look on your face."

"What *are* we celebrating?"

Luci sighed. "The good things in life, Dore."

"If caviar is one of the good things, maybe I'm not up for it."

"Of course you are. It's an acquired taste. One

that not just anybody can appreciate, of course. The truly good things in life are like that. You *do* want the truly good things in life, don't you Dore?"

Dore took another small nibble of caviar, and another swallow of champagne. In tiny bites, the caviar wasn't so bad. And the champagne tasted surprisingly good. It was almost as if she could feel the bubbles warming her up from the inside.

She didn't want Luci to think she was some kind of stooge. Luci seemed to know so much — so much that her parents had never told her, or allowed her to learn. So much that she suddenly felt she desperately needed to know.

She felt a sudden wave of hatred for her parents. For everything in her life.

She held out the champagne glass. "I think," she said, "I'm acquiring a taste for this."

Luci tilted the bottle and poured the singing bubbles into Dore's glass. "Here's to the good things," she said. "And going out and getting them."

"Here's to," echoed Dore, and drank deeply.

A few days later Dore was sitting in the bleachers after school, watching the football team practice. Randy thought she'd come because of him. He was definitely hotdogging it. But it wasn't Randy she was watching; it was Corbin.

It was Corbin she wanted.

Randy was entertaining enough, more acceptable than Tom (she smiled at *that* memory), but she was getting tired of listening to his play-by-play commentary on everything. Even — her lip curled unconsciously — even when they were steaming up the windows of the car. She was ready to move on.

And Corbin, in addition to being definitely smoother than Randy, smoother than ice on glass, was also attached to Mary.

Her glance shifted to the cheerleaders, earnestly practicing their routines on the apron of grass beyond the track that encircled the scrimmage field. Mary had her hands cupped, ordering the other cheerleaders around.

Cheerleaders! The little curl stayed in Dore's lip. She was going to spike one cheerleader's rah-rahs. She was going to make one cheerleader take notice. And be very, very unhappy.

Corbin went over to the sidelines and took off his helmet to get a drink.

Look at me, she willed him. *Look at me.*

Almost as if he heard her thoughts, he raised his head slowly. She looked down at him and shifted her position slightly, stretching her long, long legs out as if she were trying to get more comfortable. Then she smiled.

He stared at her for a moment longer. Finally, slowly, he smiled back. He tossed down the water and turned away.

But she could tell by the way he walked that he knew she was watching.

Far across the field, the cheerleaders began a series of complicated tumbles. All except one. The one who'd been calling the shots only a minute before had stopped, hands on hips, and was standing looking out across the field.

Had Mary been able to see what had just happened?

Dore hoped so.

A short time later, Dore stood waiting by the back steps of the school. It was getting late. Dark. She shivered a little in the cool evening air.

Where was Randy?

The door opened, and another stream of people came out.

Mary Moran and Corbin were among them. This time, he didn't take so long to smile back at her. He was still smiling when Mary came up and took his arm. She stood on tiptoe and kissed his cheek and began to lead him away. Dore saw Corbin look back over his shoulder. At her. She met his eyes without smiling, without blinking.

Then they were gone.

The streetlights came on. The sound of people's voices, getting into cars, leaving, drifted back to her.

Arms closed around her. Pulled her close.

Suffocatingly close.

"Randy?" She tried to turn.

But she was held in a grip of iron. A vise.

Something flashed in front of her eyes. Claws.

She tried to pull her hands free, tried to protect herself.

The claws bore down, down.

To her face.

Chapter 8

Her face was wet. Sticky.

Hands touched her cheek. She swung wildly.

"Hey. Hey!" said a familiar voice.

The giddy blackness swam away from her and she saw . . .

"Stan?"

"Shh," said Stan. "You fell. Did you trip?"

"No. Someone . . ."

"What's going on?" Randy's voice. Now in the half-light she could see him and the shadows of the last of the football players emerging from the building.

"What happened — wow. Look at her sleeve!"

And, then, suddenly, there was Gwen. Gwen was leaning over her. Gwen was helping her sit up. Dore looked up at Gwen. Then down at her arm. The sleeve of her jacket was torn. Shredded.

"You're lucky," said Stan.

"Lucky?" croaked Dore.

"That you landed on your shoulder."

"They should put better lights out here," said Gwen indignantly. "Someone might really get hurt!" Someone did, Dore wanted to say. But she wasn't. Was she?

"Are you okay?" asked Randy, echoing her thoughts.

"I . . . yes . . ." She was so confused.

"I'll take her," said Randy.

"She's fine where she is," said Stan, tightening his arm on her shoulders.

"I want to get up," she said.

It would have been funny if she hadn't felt so weak. So sick. Funny the way they both grabbed onto her, helping her up. Gwen began gathering up her books.

"C'mon," said Randy.

"I . . ."

"Dore." That was Stan.

"Stan? Stan, what are you doing here?"

"I'm the team mascot, remember? We were working out some drills. With the cheerleaders."

"Oh."

"I'll get you home," said Randy. "You just need to rest."

"Wait. Stan . . . Randy." She stopped. Moaned.

"My car is right here," said Randy.

Surprisingly, Gwen intervened. "I'll take Dore home. You guys can work this out later."

This was Gwen talking? Dore's head spun.

"Stan . . . please," she whispered. Stan let go of her arm and stepped back. "I'll call you," he said.

Beside her, Randy gave a little snort of laughter. "I'll *see* you," he said with heavy emphasis.

"C'mon, Dore," said Gwen, grabbing the arm that Stan had released. The unshredded arm.

"Okay," she said obediently.

As she let Gwen lead her to her car, she heard Randy's voice raised behind her. "She fell. What're you all waiting for? Blood?"

Suddenly, Gwen was a tower of strength. It was Gwen who got them past Dore's mother, full of cheerful greetings, happy talk. Gwen who shepherded Dore upstairs. Gwen who got something for Dore to drink and settled her in her bed.

Good old Gwen, thought Dore. She could imagine having to talk to her mother: "Dore, what happened?" "Well, Mother, guess what, something tried to claw me to death while I was waiting for Randy after football practice."

No. To her mother, that would just mean she shouldn't be going out with Randy at all. In fact, her mother didn't *know* she was going out with Randy, exactly.

Although Dore could tell she was suspicious.

No, thought Dore, I don't want Mother worrying.

Like worrying me to death. . . .

The phone began to ring as she lay back gratefully on her bed without even turning on the light.

"I'll get something to drink," Gwen had just said, slipping out.

Still feeling as if she were moving in slow motion, Dore picked up the phone.

"Dore."

"Stan." Dore sighed.

"Did you get home all right?"

"I'm home. I'm fine. Thanks for your help."

"Dore, we've got to talk."

"No, we don't."

"Randy's *not* a nice guy, Dore. Talk to some of the other girls he's gone out with. Or talk to some of his friends . . . even his friends will tell you. . . ."

"Stan, please."

"I don't understand what happened to us. One minute, we're fine. The next minute, you're gone. But that's not the issue, really. Not any more . . ."

Ignoring his words, Dore interrupted. "It was time for a change, Stan. What's so hard to understand about that?"

"Dore . . ."

"Stan, enough. Find yourself a nice girl. . . ."

Stan's voice suddenly hardened. "You should listen to me, Dore."

"You don't have anything to say that I want to hear." She hung up the phone. Hard.

And looked up to see Gwen hovering in the door.

Her face was pale. Blanched white. "W-who was it?"

"Stan the man," said Dore scornfully. "He wants to talk."

"Did he . . . did he say what about?"

"As if I didn't know." She closed her eyes. And, immediately seeing the great, gleaming claws of the beast, opened them again.

Gwen set the glasses of diet Coke by the bed. The ice rattled in the glasses like the chatter of cold teeth.

"Thanks, Gwen . . . Gwen. There's not a circus or anything in town, is there? Like with tigers in it, or anything?"

"No. Why?"

"I don't know." Dore half-closed her eyes and leaned back again. Gwen sat down on the edge of the chair. Silence settled over the room.

Dore sat up again. "Gwen. What were you still doing at the school?"

Jumping up, Gwen began to move restlessly around the room. "Oh. I had work. Had to get stuff out of my locker. I . . . hey, what's this?" Gwen held up the silver mirror.

Had Dore left it out? She didn't remember doing that. "It's a mirror," she said shortly. Was Gwen changing the subject?

Gwen tilted the mirror and studied her face in it. "It's heavy. Funny, too. What . . . odd . . . decorations."

"It's old." Now Gwen was making her jumpy. What if she dropped the mirror? Why didn't she just go away?

As if she were reading her mind, Gwen put down the mirror on the desk with a little clunk. "If you're feeling okay, I'll go on."

"Great . . . I mean, thanks and all, but I'm okay now. I'll just chill for a while."

"Yeah. Well. See ya. You want me to turn out the light?"

"Yes. Thanks."

Dore closed her eyes as Gwen left. She heard her footsteps go down the stairs, heard the front door close. Then she opened her eyes again and stared up into the darkness. *Had* she fallen? And, unconscious, imagined the whole thing?

No. It had been real. Real. It had been waiting for her in the dark. Something had come for her out of the shadows.

The darkness in her room suddenly felt eerie and cold. She got up, carefully but quickly, and turned on the lamp. Her hands were still shaking.

"Reality check," she murmured, and sank into the chair next to the bookcase.

No such thing as a beast. No.

The phone rang. She picked it up quickly.

"What's happening?"

"Luci. Hi."

"I didn't know beauty queens ever fell," said Luci. "I thought you had practice in all that sort of thing."

"Word travels fast," answered Dore. "But I didn't fall."

"What happened?"

Dore hesitated. It was so wild. *A wild beast.*

"Well . . . I don't know."

Luci let it go. "You okay now?"

"Fine. No big deal." Trust Luci to keep her curiosity contained, she thought wryly. Dore's eyes fell on her jacket, wadded on the floor by her closet. "Tore my jacket."

"Tough," said Luci sympathetically. "Well, listen, if you need anything."

"Right," said Dore.

"Later," said Luci, and hung up.

Going over to the closet, Dore picked up the jacket. One arm was shredded. Not ripped, or scraped apart, or anything that might have happened in a fall.

Torn to ribbons.

"Damn," said Dore. It could have been her skin. Her skin hanging in bloody strips. Her skin, peeled back to the bone.

Her face.

Hastily she pushed the jacket to the back of her closet. She'd sneak it out the next day, before her mother or Mrs. Bauer found it.

She never wanted to see it again.

For the first time since she'd come in, she became aware of her reflection in the mirrors. She leaned closer.

The claws hadn't touched her face. She was safe.

Picking up the mirror where Gwen had left it, Dore examined her face more closely.

A hideous scar ran from her temple to her chin. It was as white as the belly of a dead fish, with that same gruesome iridescence. It pulled the skin of her face sideways, making one eye wild and skewed. The mouth on the face in the mirror gaped open. Breath fogged the mirror, hiding the face. . . .

The face of a beast.

Chapter 9

No.

No. Her hand jerked with the shock of it, and
now her own face looked back at her. It was just a
trick of the light, nothing more.

She smiled. If Luci hadn't given her the mirror,
she would have thought it was one of Stan's special
effects, like his fake blood.

Stan. Slowly her smile faded. Stan. What was it
about Stan? Something . . . something she couldn't
quite put together.

Like what was Stan doing at the school at that
time? Practicing with the cheerleaders, he'd said.
But she would have seen him. And she hadn't. No.
No, wait, what were Stan and Gwen doing at the
school at that time of night?

And why had Gwen been so shaky about that
phone call from Stan?

"I have something to tell you." Wasn't that what
Stan said?

Stan. And Gwen. Stan and Gwen.

That was it!

Gwen, with her big, sickening worried act. When all she was really worried about was whether Dore knew about her and Stan. About how she had *stolen* Stan from Dore.

Stan and Gwen. Gwen and Stan.

"Surprise, surprise, surprise," muttered Dore. "Surprise, Gwen. . . ."

"Gwen."

Gwen jumped. "Oh! Dore!"

"Where've you been?" asked Dore. "I thought you'd at least be around to ask me how I was doing." *How are you doing, Gwen? You and Stan?*

"Me? Oh. How are you?" Gwen was staring at Dore as if mesmerized.

"Fine. Thanks so much for all your help, Gwen."

"No problem."

Dore slid onto the bench next to Gwen. It was a beautiful day, and the seniors were grabbing onto senior privileges, eating lunch outside. Gwen, of course, had copped a table that was mostly in the shade. But Dore settled in a patch of sun and lifted her face to it. It felt good. It'd be nice to know how to purr, she thought. Not that she liked cats. They were too independent. But then dogs were so needy.

Speaking of needy dogs, she couldn't let herself forget why she was talking to Gwen. She opened her eyes wide and smiled. "I've been taking it easy, anyway. But, you know, we really haven't been seeing too much of each other." She lowered her voice. "It's Randy. I mean, I thought it was the real thing, y'know?"

"Ahhm," was all Gwen could manage.

"But it isn't. Oh, Gwen." Dore sighed.

"I'm sorry," said Gwen. But she looked more worried, more *guilty* than sorry, in spite of the sympathy Dore's words had obviously conjured up.

"Well, we're not dead yet, exactly. But you know how it is." She waited, but Gwen didn't say anything. Dore looked down and laced her fingers together. "Anyway, at least I'll have more time to spend with my friends. And my work."

"Oh."

"But I need your help, Gwen."

"Anything," said Gwen.

That's better, thought Dore. She looked through her lashes at her oldest friend. Her *former* best friend. "Well, I hate to ask, but . . . listen, Gwen, could you lend me your English notes? We've got that killer test tomorrow, and I haven't exactly studied. And I haven't exactly been paying attention in class, either. You know. . . ."

Slowly Gwen nodded. "I guess I could. But you'd have to give them back to me first thing tomorrow. I'll need to review them at lunch."

"Of *course*," said Dore. "Thanks, Gwen. I knew I could count on you. After all, what are best friends for?"

Ducking her head, Gwen began to paw through her backpack without answering.

Dore looked around. Randy, she knew, was somewhere out in the parking lot, grossing it up with the other jocks. Corbin was hooked onto Mary somewhere. At the far table, in the sun, she saw Carol and Luci and half a dozen other girls laughing and talking. She'd go over and join them in just a minute — just as soon as Gwen finished fiddling around in that backpack.

"You know," said Dore idly, "I haven't seen Stan around lately. . . ."

Gwen jumped, and the backpack slid from her hands, scattering papers all around.

Dore reached out instinctively, catching a bulky package among the papers.

"No!" cried Gwen, snatching the package. "I'll take care of it." With the package clutched under one arm, she dropped to her knees and began to scramble desperately at Dore's feet, scooping papers up and dropping them in the backpack. "Here," she said. "Here's the notebook. You'll find everything without any problem. Just don't . . . don't forget to give this back to me tomorrow morning."

"On the steps, first thing," agreed Dore.

"Gotta go," gasped Gwen.

Dore didn't turn to watch Gwen disappear.

She had what she wanted.

"Hi, Randy," said Dore neutrally. She was on the phone in her room.

Randy sounded definitely stoned. What a bore. Holding the phone, Dore began to get undressed while he rambled, dropping her clothes over the chair. She walked over to her closet, enjoying the feel of air against her bare skin, and pulled out a pale blue silk bathrobe. That felt good against her skin, too. She left the sash untied — why not have it all? she thought.

"That's nice, Randy," she said. She sat down at her desk and pulled Gwen's notebook toward her. Oscar Wilde. Ugh. But at least she wouldn't have to read everything he wrote. She knew from past experience that Gwen's notes would be exhaustive, and that she'd have the teacher's words down verbatim.

"Really?" said Dore, running her eyes down the page. Blah, blah, blah.

And there it was. Glaring confirmation. Stan's name written over and over in the margin of one of the pages.

Stan and Gwen.

And what was this? A note, folded end over end. Dore unfolded it.

Gwen — can't wait. Love, Stan.

A love note.

And even though she'd known, even though she no longer wanted Stan, she was furious all over again. More furious than she'd ever been in her life.

"Listen, Randy," she said abruptly, "I've got to go. Something . . . something important has come up. Yes. No. Later, okay? Okay."

She hung up, her thoughts seething, her blood burning with rage.

Stan and Gwen. Gwen and Stan.

Dore's lip curled. Vegetarian sex, she thought, if there was such a thing. Boring boy, boring girl, boring sex. . . .

Gwen was going to pay. And Stan. But Gwen first. And most.

She realized that the note was crumpled in her hand. She dropped the wad of paper in the wastebasket.

Which was exactly where she was going to put Gwen.

Chapter 10

Last and proud of it, thought Dore, sliding into a seat in the front of her English class just as the bell finished ringing. Mr. Garrigle, aka the Gargoyle, tried to melt her into a guilty, cringing puddle with his bug-eyes. Dore fluttered her own eyelids and topped it off with a centerfold smile, and it was the Gargoyle who looked away.

No contest, Mr. Garrigle. She rested her chin on her fingers and kept staring. That's entertainment, Mr. G, she thought. And it helped distract her from another set of laser eyes.

Gwen's.

Because somewhere near the back of the room, where she usually sat with Dore, Gwen sat alone. Staring.

The Gargoyle stood up, picked up the stack of test questions, put them down, wiped his hands on his pants, and picked them up again. He went from row to row, handing the test papers to the first person in each row. When he reached Dore's row, she let her fingers slide along his.

He started and dropped the papers.

"Oh, I'm *so* sorry," murmured Dore. She shifted her legs to one side, letting her skirt slide up a little more. But the Gargoyle kept his head determinedly down as he gathered the papers back up and again handed them, very, very carefully, to Dore.

Turning to pass the stack of tests along as Mr. Garrigle began to go over the test rules, Dore took a quick look at Gwen.

Yes. Gwen was sitting stiff as a corpse. And staring at Dore like a zombie.

"You may begin," concluded Mr. Garrigle.

Dore glanced down at the test questions. Piece of cake. Gwen's notes, as always, had been excellent.

Too bad when she'd finished with them, she'd had to throw them away.

"Too bad," said Dore. She kept walking, despite Gwen's hand on her arm.

"That test was one third of our grade! One *third!*"

"I know. That's why I needed your notes."

"You promised you'd give them back before school. I waited on the front steps until I was almost late for homeroom — "

"Woo-woo," murmured Dore.

" — and you never showed up. I've been trying to find you all day."

"I've been busy." Dore stopped at her locker,

threw some stuff inside, and slammed it shut. She looked up.

Gwen was waiting expectantly.

"You're still here?"

"I can't believe you'd do this!"

"You think you flunked, Gwen?"

"I know I did. Thanks to *you*."

"Good."

Gwen's mouth dropped open. Gasping, she finally choked out, "Fine! Fine. Just give me my notebook, and that's that, Dore. I am *through*."

"You certainly are," answered Dore. She turned and walked away.

Then she stopped. Before Gwen could say anything, Dore added, "Tell me, Gwen. What *did* you have to do to get Stan to follow you home?"

She didn't stay to admire the horrified, stricken look on Gwen's face.

It's just the beginning, Gwen, thought Dore. Get used to it.

"Look at this!" Luci unceremoniously pushed Dore's soda to one side, and slapped the magazine down in front of her.

"Hey!"

"Look," insisted Luci.

"I have been looking," Dore complained.

They were hanging out in Pryo's Gyros, along with half the school.

"Well?"

Dore gave a gusty, exaggerated sigh. "I know I

said I was going to the library, Luci, but it doesn't mean I have to *read* anything."

"Exert yourself this one time."

Dore lifted the magazine and examined a photograph of a model. "I'd never wear this, not in a million years. It's strictly photo-shoot. Public relations rags, you know?"

"Not the pic. READ."

Dore read a movie blurb about a hot new movie, starring Cane Adams. She almost said, "So what?" Almost, almost. She frowned.

Then she saw it.

"No way," she breathed. "An unknown . . ."

"An unknown," emphasized Luci. "Just like in *Gone With the Wind*. They want new talent. You could do it in a second. All you have to do is show up for the audition."

Dore gave herself a moment to think about it all: not the crummy cattle calls of beauty pageants, not having to wear out her face smiling at nobody judges with hypocritical morals ogling her in her bathing suit and breathing on her after it was over. No more living in the middle of nowhere, with every moment planned into the future.

Freedom. Instead, freedom.

She could be a star.

And if the photo of this girl they were using as an example was representative of the competition, it would be a snap.

"You'll have to skip a little school," Luci pointed out. "It's a long drive from here."

"No problem," said Dore, closing the magazine carefully. "Are you going to try out?"

She expected Luci to say no. For some reason, she expected Luci not to be interested.

But Luci shrugged, and didn't answer. Then she smiled, and it seemed to Dore that she had the larger-than-life glow of a star. A dark star. A star who could ruin Dore's dreams.

I could beat Luci, thought Dore. But she remembered then the first time she'd met Luci, the magnetism, the heat that Luci had given off.

Suddenly she wasn't so sure.

Suddenly, Dore wanted Luci gone.

Her eyes met Luci's and for one unsettling moment, Dore was sure that Luci could read her thoughts. Then Luci tipped her head slightly. "Low-flying Corbin coming on your left," she murmured.

Dore pushed the magazine into her pack as Luci said, "Hi, Corbin. You here alone?"

How did Luci know Corbin?

"Well . . ." Corbin stopped by their booth, smiling. Dore tilted her chin up and looked into his eyes. She was a sucker for green eyes, no question about it.

"I'm meeting Mary," he said.

"Mary Moran?" asked Luci, frowning.

Corbin shrugged. "Who else?"

"How lucky — to spend *all* your free time with Mary."

"Well," said Corbin.

And then Mary appeared. "Corbin," she said, and

fastened both hands around his upper arm.

Corbin looked annoyed.

"Hello," Mary said flatly, without looking directly at either Luci or Dore.

"Hi, Mary," said Dore, as sweetly as she knew how. She smiled again at Corbin.

"C'mon." Mary gave Corbin's arm a tug, as if he were on a leash.

Corbin definitely looked annoyed, but he allowed himself to be shepherded toward a booth in the corner, where the cheerleaders and the jocks were at play.

Dore's expression changed from one of sweetness to one of rueful understanding.

And Corbin winked.

"Progress," declared Luci. "Major progress."

Dore said, "Major progress is when Mary disappears. . . ."

"Hmmm." Luci pulled to a stop in front of Dore's house. "How?"

"Can you die of embarrassment? I'd like to embarrass Mary to death. It'd serve her right."

"You'll think of something," said Luci.

Dore thought of Gwen.

"I know," said Dore.

Chapter 11

The car screamed down on the girl at impossible speed.

She never had a chance.

The wheels crushed her body. Flat.

They crushed the body of the boy who was with her.

They crushed the body of the elephant, too.

Then the car drove a lap around the field, the tiger behind the wheel waving demonically.

At the end of halftime, while the cheerleaders picked up the dummies of the rival team's cheerleader, football player, and mascot, who had been crushed by the car, Carol said, "You have to hand it to Stan. He puts on a great show."

"Mmm," said Dore.

"So," said Carol, slyly, "where's Gwen? I expected to see her here tonight."

"Didn't you talk to her?" asked Dore offhandedly.

"She's been looking a little out of it," put in Luci.

Not as out of it as she's going to be, thought Dore. "Here they come!" she said.

"Randy's doing a *great* job," said Carol as they all jumped up with the rest of the crowd, cheering.

Down below, Dore watched Mary herky jump like a mad Chihuahua.

She watched the tiger mascot come bounding out to join the cheerleaders.

She smiled.

Rice's wasn't exactly jumping. It wasn't that kind of a store. The floors were old, dark wood. Tall mirrors and comfortable chairs were scattered at discreet intervals around the floor, interspersed with rich cherry wood paneling. Everywhere you looked there was space and comfort, uncluttered by the racks and racks of clothes found at department stores.

But, then, when you had the best, you didn't need the rest.

"Thanks, Chanelle." Taking the dresses she'd chosen from the attending saleswoman, Dore went into the dressing room.

She'd boosted her mother's credit card. She was looking for something a future star might wear.

A voice from a nearby dressing room stopped her in mid-undress.

"Ohh. It's just right." Gwen.

"It looks lovely, sweetie." Gwen's mother.

"Taking it up to that hem length was an excellent idea, miss."

Dore heard the door open and knew that Gwen had gone out to view the dress at one of the larger three-way mirrors.

"Your first dance. Oh, dear. You're growing up."

"Oh, Mom, I'm so excited."

"You and Stan will make a charming couple, darling. . . . Come on, now, let's go see about some shoes."

"Oh, Mom!"

Dore struck a pose in front of the mirror, chin on laced fingers, eyes wide. The photographers at the pageants had loved that look. So innocent.

Your first dance, Gwen? Try your last.

Dore went back to her dresses. It wasn't easy. Before, there had been colors that hadn't looked right, cuts that, even on her, were not the best. But these days, everything she touched seemed made for her. She lingered lovingly over each one, finally choosing a sleek, sophisticated short silk suit, in winter white, for the audition.

Her mother would croak when she got the bill. But so what?

The white would look innocent, she decided. It made her feel sort of kinky.

And, now, she thought, *something for the dance.* Randy hadn't asked her yet. But he would. And Corbin would be there. And then . . . anything could happen.

For the dance she chose a blood-red dress, which covered her from neck to hem, with long sleeves. And fit like paint.

She'd never been able to wear that color before. Or felt quite right in that style.

But, now . . .

"Corbin, here I come," she told her reflection.

She was paying for the clothes when the name on a dress hanging on an alteration rack caught her eye.

Mary Moran.

"Oh!" she exclaimed, pointing. "May I see that one?"

"It's been sold, miss," said Chanelle.

"I know. But couldn't I just see it? Please." The look worked on salesclerks as well as on anyone else. A moment later, Chanelle was reverently lifting the dress out of the bag.

So that was what Mary was wearing.

She had decent taste, Dore acknowledged grudgingly. Aloud she said, "How does it work? It wraps. Oh, I see! How clever. It's all one piece, really.

"It's for the Silver and Gold Dance, isn't it? Yes, of course, I know Mary Moran. That color *blue* is just right for her. It's a perfect dress."

Chanelle looked gratified. "Yes, miss, it is, isn't it? Although," she added hastily, restoring the dress to the garment bag, "your dress is stunning."

"Yes," said Dore. But she wasn't thinking about her dress.

She was thinking about Mary's.

She could hardly wait for the dance.

But she had a few things to take care of first.

* * *

"Anyone ever tell you you're a fox?"

"Never," she whispered, running the tip of one finger down Randy's earlobe. Funny that a jock could be so turned on by having his earlobe touched. "I can hardly wait for the dance."

"Yeah," he breathed, pulling her to him hard. "Sure . . ."

A fox, she thought scornfully that night in her room, after her date with Randy. She considered doing her exercises.

"No," she said aloud, remembering the last part of the evening with Randy. "I've had enough exercise tonight." His name certainly suited him. . . .

Besides, she'd never looked so good. Everyone said so. Even Carol the gossip, who was hard put to say anything plain nice about a person, had said just yesterday that Dore was definitely the most beautiful girl in the whole school.

Of course, with Carol, it could be a put-down. After all, it wasn't that big a school. So big deal, right?

Dore's eyes went to the calendar on her desk. She'd drawn a red heart around the date of the audition. Just that. No sense in leaving clues around for her nosy parents. They'd just try to find some way to stop her. No, it was all set. Only she and Luci knew.

Most beautiful at Eleanor Roosevelt. That was a laugh. Who in hell cared?

It wasn't enough. It wasn't nearly enough.

She wanted to own the world.

* * *

Saturday morning and Mrs. Bauer was serving breakfast. Dore's mother, as usual on Saturday mornings, was in her room, "catching up on my beauty sleep." Her father, as usual any morning, was reading.

Dore, not as usual, was thumbing through the morning newspaper, looking for an article about the movie and the tryouts. Nothing in the first section. Nothing in the art and society section. Dore frowned. Business, maybe?

Finishing a vain hunt through the entire paper, even the sports section, Dore pushed it aside and found herself being scrutinized by her father.

Also not as usual.

"What?" said Dore.

"School project?" asked her father.

"Mmm." Parents were so nosy. "More coffee?" She motioned for Mrs. Bauer to refill her own cup.

"Thank you," said her father to Mrs. Bauer. But he kept frowning at Dore.

"Call out the wrinkle squad, Dad. You're looking pretty serious."

Her father ignored her. Naturally. "You — there's something different about you, Dore."

You bet there is. "Just growing up, I guess." Dore suddenly felt uncomfortable under her father's examination. It was the same sort of examination he gave to the horned caterpillars or whatever those things were that ate his tomatoes in the garden.

Her father didn't look convinced.

"Could you stop staring?"

He still didn't listen. Instead, he shook his head slowly. "I can't quite put my finger on it."

Dore said quickly, "Is there something wrong with my face?"

"No," said her father. "In fact, I've never seen you look so . . . beautiful."

Her father wasn't one to sling compliments around. In fact, he wasn't one to notice anything about her at all. Feeling pleased in spite of herself, she said, "Thanks, Dad."

"Don't thank me. It's not necessarily an achievement. . . ."

Dore pushed his voice out of her mind as he shifted into his lecture mode. She'd never looked better. And that was the truth. The only truth.

Just then, a horn sounded, a long, impatient wail.

Her father's attention shifted abruptly. "God in heaven, what's that noise? Sounded like the last trumpet."

"It's just Luci. We're going to the library."

Her father shifted his frown back to her, but she was ready.

"School project," she said. "See ya."

"Dore — " she heard him say, but she kept going. That was the important thing — to keep moving.

Parents, she thought again, running out the front door to Luci's Miata.

Luci was revving away almost before Dore got the door closed.

"Hey! Are you trying to kill me?"

"Nah," said Luci.

She had the top up, but all the windows were down, even though it was a cold morning.

"It's colder'n hell in here," Dore complained.

Luci turned to face Dore, her long red hair whipping around her face like fire. "Nah!" she said cheerfully. "But turn on the heat."

Bending down, Dore punched the heat up to high. Then she pushed the play button on the CD player. Music howled through the car, words about being pleased to meet you and guessing someone's name. . . .

"What's this?" Dore called above the music.

"An oldie. By the Stones. One of my favorites." Luci threw her own head back, as if she might howl, too, then floored the accelerator. Dore was thrown back against the seat as if the car had just shot into orbit.

And suddenly she wished they were. "Faster!" she demanded, throwing her own head back. "Faster."

"Watch this!" Luci pulled up behind a station wagon, slowing down for just a moment as they headed into a blind curve. Then she whipped out to the left and pulled even with the station wagon, dogging it, side by side.

Dore saw the other car first. "Look out!" she screamed.

But Luci never looked at all.

They were all going to die. . . .

Chapter 12

Dore saw the terrified eyes of the passengers in the other car, the open mouths screaming, screaming. . . .

A voice she didn't recognize as her own cried, "Stop! Stop! *Luciiii!*"

Luci's answer was to put the heel of one hand on the horn, keeping the other hand draped casually over the steering wheel.

The other car swerved wildly.

Looking back as they shot around the curve, Dore saw the station wagon bucking along the shoulder, fighting to stay on the road, to keep from going over and over and over into the gully below.

Luci didn't look back. Instead, she turned to Dore, smiling. "Crazy drivers . . ." she said.

"We could've been killed!"

Red-hot spots of color burned along Luci's cheeks. The smile she turned on Dore was mesmerizing, blinding. "No way," she said. "Not *us*."

For one moment, Dore was angry. For one moment, she almost demanded that Luci stop the car and let her out. For one crucial moment, she almost told Luci she'd had it.

Then she looked at her shaking hands, at Luci's bright smile — and started to laugh.

It shouldn't have been funny, but it was. And Dore couldn't stop laughing. This was life. This was life in the fast lane.

"Faster," she crowed, and turned to watch the sunburned blacktop racing toward them.

And, then, suddenly, there it was. Luci downshifted and the car screamed down to the speed limit in front of Eleanor Roosevelt. She swept her arm wide, as if offering Dore a kingdom.

"Wouldja look at that," Dore breathed.

"Guess the girls must need new uniforms," said Luci.

It was the cheerleaders, in sweatshirts and cutoffs and suds, beneath a banner that proclaimed "CAR WASH — $5.00 donation."

Dore saw Mary Moran instantly.

"Supporting our local cheerleaders," mocked Luci as she turned down the half-circle drive in front of the school and pulled to a stop by the front steps.

She leaned on the horn.

"Hey!" someone exclaimed.

Smiling, Luci kept her hand on the horn.

Hands on her hips, Mary Moran marched up to Luci. "Stop it!" she ordered.

Slowly Luci lifted her hand. "My car needs washing."

"That'll be five dollars."

"After the car wash," Luci answered.

Mary's face flushed, but she motioned them forward. "C'mon, then. Roll up your windows."

In another minute, half the squad was rubbing down the Miata.

Cocking her head, Luci said, "I like them better as car-washers."

The car gave a lurch. Dore heard a shriek and a ripping sound.

"Are you crazy!" Mary Moran cried.

This time Luci did look back. "Oops," she said.

Dore looked back, too. Mary Moran was struggling futilely to free her shirt from the car's rear flip-top hinge. The lurch of the car had torn Mary's shirt open and half off.

"Oh, dear," said Luci, rolling down her window and looking out. "I'm *so* sorry."

"You — you witch. You bimbo, you . . ."

"Will the real Mary please stand up," murmured Dore, watching the other cheerleaders rush to Mary's side. At last the sleeve was free.

Dore caught a glimpse of herself in the side mirror and saw that she was smiling — until Mary's face loomed up in the window. When her shirt had gotten caught, she'd let go of the hose and gotten drenched as well. Her hair was plastered to her head, and water streaked her face.

But the water hadn't cooled her off.

"You'll pay for this!" Mary shrieked.

Luci laughed. "You're all wet, Mary," she said.

And Dore joined in Luci's laughter as they peeled away in a spray of water.

Dore paused in the door of the packed gym and surveyed the crowd with a practiced eye. It was all so — high school — that she had to stifle a yawn. Of course, being there with Randy, Mr. Studley himself, didn't help.

Thank God she'd soon be out of there, and not with Randy. And soon she'd be on her way to the top of the world. Meanwhile, she was going to have some fun.

"C'mon, babe." Randy caught her hand and pulled her into the crowd. She felt his hands sliding down the back of her dress and sighed inwardly. Part of the fun — without any doubt, part of the fun — was going to be dumping Randy. Publicly.

Public humiliation. Yes. The idea of it definitely gave her a little thrill. Thinking about it, she wriggled a little closer to Randy, deftly shifting his hand out of what he probably thought was the erotic zone, and positioned herself so she could see over his shoulder.

A shimmering flash of copper caught her eye in the strobe light, and she knew instinctively that Luci was dancing nearby. But she had too much on her mind to think about Luci. Not now.

The DJ, probably on the signal of some uptight teacher, swung into something fast, and Dore and

Randy broke apart. Dancing with jocklike determination, Randy flashed the leer he thought was a sexy smile. Dore looked past him, scanning the body count for a blue dress and Corbin's white-hot grin.

But not yet. Not yet.

Who she did see was Stan. Stan and Gwen. They'd stopped dancing, and their heads were together. Gwen made a gesture, and Stan nodded, his hand cupped under her elbow.

Dore stopped dancing abruptly.

"Excuse me," she said, and made her way across the floor and out through the gym doors.

The girls' locker room was almost empty. Earlier, it would have been full of people checking their dresses. Later, it would be full of girls who'd had too much to drink, or were full of gossip, or just taking a break or an illicit smoke out of sight of the chaperones.

Taking her time, Dore strolled down the long row of shadowy lockers and took a seat on one of the benches.

A few minutes later, Gwen bustled in.

Dore waited until Gwen was almost to the bathroom door. "What's your hurry, Gwen?"

Gwen froze. Turned. "Dore?"

"Your old friend."

Gwen raised her chin defiantly. "What do you want?"

"To share. Merely to share . . ."

Without speaking, Gwen peered at Dore uncertainly.

"I wanted to share a little discovery I made . . . about Stan."

"What?" Gwen asked sharply.

"Gwen, dearest. You know that night I fell? After football practice? I didn't fall, Gwen. I was pushed. I was pushed by someone who attacked me."

"S-so?"

"Who was it? That would be the normal question. But you don't ask. Which makes me think you know. Don't you?"

"No."

"Yes. Stan. Stan, with all his special effects and weird tricks done with mirrors. Stan the magician. Stan, who's gotten just a little — too — weird."

"No!" said Gwen.

"Yes," said Dore again, pensively. "I wonder why? Jealousy? Revenge . . . maybe the same reason he is going out with you. Stan's got a mean streak, Gwen, make no mistake."

"It's not true. I *know* it's not true."

"Well, he sure wasn't out there practicing a new stunt. I would've seen him. And why else would he lie?"

"He — you — you're the liar! You. You're just saying this to hurt Stan. And me."

Dore shook her head.

"You are. Well, I won't let you get away with it, Dore. You'll be sorry. . . ."

Dore stood up. And Gwen stepped forward.

Instinctively, Dore moved back.

Almost like an animal, Gwen bared her teeth.

"You are despicable. Loathsome. You — "

"Why? Because I told you the truth? Maybe you don't want to hear it, but I bet there are others who would."

"You wouldn't dare."

"Wouldn't I?" Dore walked by Gwen and turned to face her. "You're right. Maybe I wouldn't. But there'll be a price, Gwennie. I'll let you know what it is."

Dore walked casually out of the locker room as two girls came in the door. She didn't look back, didn't hear the little hiss that escaped between Gwen's bared teeth. Nor did she hear the soft words: "Oh, you'll get paid. I promise. . . ."

Chapter 13

Fun, fun, fun.

Having so much fun that she didn't notice Gwen come out to the edge of the dance floor, didn't notice her motion to Stan. She didn't notice them leaving.

It was as if someone had given her the whole world. She felt as if she owned it, anyway. She felt so strong, so powerful. She could have, she *knew* she could have, anything she wanted.

And the fun was only beginning.

She reached out for Randy and pulled him across the floor. He came willingly. By the time the music stopped, she was close to Mary and Corbin.

Dore caught Corbin's eye and raised her eyebrows half-mockingly. Then she looked at Mary's dress. It was tied in a big bow on the back of Mary's neck, the ends streaming down almost to her knees.

"What's a nice girl like you doing in a place like this?"

Turning, Dore found Luci at her side. Luci was wearing an orange dress that no red-headed person should have been able to wear. But on Luci, it looked outrageously right — and outrageously wrong. Luci's dress did *not* look like a high school dance.

"Dancing," said Dore.

"Having fun?"

A little smile curled Dore's lips. "Def. Most def."

"Well, I was admiring the view. He *is* gorgeous, isn't he?"

Dore considered asking Luci what she meant, but Luci wouldn't fall for that. She glanced quickly at Randy. No problem. He and Luci's date were yukking it up like three-year-olds in a sandbox.

"Not bad," admitted Dore. "So?"

"Well, you've had fun with the rest — why not have fun with the best?"

Dore shook her head. Having Luci, assertive, self-confident Luci, ask her what she was going to do felt good. Luci would be impressed, to say the very least, with what Dore had in mind.

"You think?" Dore countered.

The music began to pump again.

"I know," said Luci.

Randy caught Dore's arm. What a Neanderthal, thought Dore.

As if she sensed something — Corbin's wandering interest, her own vulnerability — Mary was dancing wildly now. Others had caught the spirit, too. The bodies writhed and gyrated in the flickering light, shape-changers, monstrous contortionists, leaping, leering. . . .

Dore shuddered and half turned. She was not one of them. She didn't belong there.

Then Mary flung her arms wide and, like a dervish, spun up to Corbin and caught his hand, spinning out and back.

The movement caught Dore's attention. Her eyes met Corbin's for just an instant.

Then Mary flung her hands around Corbin's neck. He automatically put his hands around her waist. Looking up soulfully at him, Mary let her hands slide down his arms, then bent backwards, throwing her arms out as she went into a deep dip.

Corbin almost fell.

Someone gave a little shriek.

And Dore stepped firmly on the very end of one of the trailing ties on Mary's dress.

Corbin jerked upright, trying to regain his balance, bringing Mary with him. The bow held for just a second, pulling Mary slightly back. Corbin's arms instinctively tightened on her, pulling her to him.

Dore spun toward Randy, quickly, deftly hooking her foot in the tie. She felt it give.

Someone else shrieked. A much louder shriek this time. Then someone else cried, "Look!"

Randy stopped dancing and turned his leer up to high.

Dore turned. Slowly.

Mary's dress had completely unwound and was hanging in big, loose swaths around her. She was desperately catching at it, trying to bring it up to cover her, but the way the dress was made, the long, long length of silk material, made it impossible for her to do anything without completely unwinding the dress and starting over.

The dancers around Mary stopped. Someone began to laugh.

Corbin reached out to try to help Mary.

"Let go of me!" she cried. "Get away from me!"

The murmurs and laughter spread throughout the gym. More and more people began to press forward to take a look at Mary Moran in her boring beige underwear.

"Stop it, stop it, stop!" Doubling over, Mary made one more vain attempt to pull her dress back around her. As she straightened up, she saw Dore.

"You!" snarled Mary.

Too bad she isn't at least wearing black lingerie. Or *something* sexy. Pantyhose. Ugh . . . Dore let her gaze move up slowly to meet Mary's. Then she looked past Mary to Corbin.

Once again, Corbin reached out to try to help Mary.

Mary's face contorted. She jerked her arm away and swung around, raising her hand.

The sound of her palm meeting Corbin's face echoed through the gym. Everyone stopped. Everyone waited to see what would happen next. Corbin didn't move.

Mary took a step toward Corbin. "Corbin, I . . ."

Corbin took a careful step back.

"Corbin?" she said thinly.

Corbin tightened his jaw and deliberately looked away.

Mary gasped, then gathering up the folds of her dress as best she could, fled toward the bathroom. The sound of the gym doors closing behind her cut off the echoes of her sobs.

Not such a great rear view, either, thought Dore. She'd never cut it in the bathing suit competition.

People began to move again. Giggles and gossip spiraled upward.

"Did you see *that*?" asked Randy.

Corbin was standing still, looking stunned. Dore smiled a little to herself.

Reaching up, she put one finger under Randy's chin and closed his mouth. "Good-bye, Randy," she said. And walked across the floor to Corbin.

"You can't do this."

Stan slid from the shadows in the corridor.

Dore kept walking. She was on her way to meet Corbin. The dance was still mega-decibel behind her. But Corbin was getting his car, and she was getting in it, and she was leaving.

She hadn't had *all* her fun for the evening.

Stan put his arm out and blocked her way without quite touching her. Almost, she thought, as if he were afraid of me. Good.

"You can't do this, Dore."

"I can do whatever I want. Move."

"Why are you saying those things about me, Dore? You know I'd never hurt you."

"It was you, Stan. Don't try to deny it."

"You told everybody you fell. In the dark."

"But I didn't. You know that. I know that. Gwen knows that. Now."

Suddenly Stan grabbed her shoulders. "Stop it, Dore! What's gotten into you? You used to be such a nice girl."

"Nice girls finish last, Stan. And you're — hurting me."

Abruptly Stan released her. "It wasn't me, Dore."

"So you admit someone attacked me? Hmm?"

"Leave it alone, Dore."

"Or what? I'll be sorry?" She started to laugh.

Shaking his head, Stan turned and walked away.

"Stan?"

He looked back.

"I'll never be sorry again, Stan."

The sounds of the dance faded behind her as she reached the brightly lit entrance hall. One of the chaperones tilted in a chair against the far wall by the ticket table. He looked asleep.

A sound stopped her. She twisted around. "Stan?"

No. Nobody. Or was there?

She turned resolutely and hurried toward the doors. The entrance hall looked garish. It smelled the smell of old schools. She hated it. She was ready to leave.

Corbin's car was easing down the rows of cars

toward the entrance. Too far away to see the figure that sprang out of the shadows.

But some instinct made Dore turn.

She didn't have time to scream, didn't have time to do anything.

Clawing hands snatched at Dore's dress. Dore twisted sideways. The figure followed, grabbing Dore in a grotesque dance. Dore felt hot breath against her neck. She hit the figure. Hard. Harder. Then it was tumbling end over end, falling like a rag doll to the foot of the stairs, into the well of darkness that pooled beside them there.

Gasping, Dore peered down the stairs. Nothing moved as Corbin pulled to a stop below.

"Die," whispered Dore. Then she walked slowly down the stairs. Slowly — she didn't want Corbin to think he'd have it easy.

Slowly, to still the pounding of her heart. To keep watching the still dark shape below.

Was it moving?

Slowly still, she walked past it and across the broad sidewalk where Corbin waited.

Soon she'd be leaving. Soon, none of this would matter.

It wasn't her fault, was it?

No. Not her fault. Not her responsibility.

She settled into Corbin's car languidly. Could he hear the pounding of her heart?

Could he see the figure at the bottom of the stairs?

He couldn't. "Where to?" he asked, his voice lazy, amused.

"Anywhere you want to go," she answered, matching her voice to his.

They pulled away, leaving it all behind.

Dore never saw the second figure come out of the building behind her.

Never saw it start to make its own leisurely way down the stairs.

Chapter 14

Dore picked up the phone on the second ring.

"God, Luci, I *am* wasted. And was it ever worth it. . . ."

But it wasn't Luci's voice that answered.

"Murderer," the voice breathed. "You killed her."

Dore slammed down the phone. It wasn't possible. "I can handle this," she said aloud and was ready when the phone rang again.

Dore picked it up on the first ring this time. "Listen, I'm warning you. . . ."

"Dore?"

"Stan?" Dore leaned back.

"Dore, Gwen's dead."

For a moment, Dore didn't breathe. Didn't move. "Dead?" she whispered at last. "It's not possible."

"She fell. Down the back stairs at school."

"Oh, Stan." Dore heard her own voice, hollow, flat. Did Stan hear how false she sounded? "What happened? Do you know?"

"No. She was . . . Dore. Listen. You know what happened to you that night?"

"When you pushed me? Are you saying you pushed Gwen?"

"No! I never . . . it wasn't me. The stairs were dark. She must've tripped."

Dore kept her voice even. "If that's what you want to be the official version, Stan."

His voice suddenly thinned in anger. "I can't believe you, Dore. Gwen is dead. Dead. Your oldest, your best friend. And all you can do is . . ."

"Blame you, Stan. It's your fault," said Dore. "Think about it!"

She slammed down the phone. Then she threw it. She pulled the sheets up around her and tried to dive back into sleep.

Who could possibly know what had happened? No one.

And it wasn't her fault. Gwen had tried to kill *her*. And Gwen had taken the fall she deserved.

That was all.

Wasn't it?

The phone rang again, almost immediately.

She picked it up. She waited without speaking.

Carol's voice said, "Your line was busy."

"Uh-huh," she answered noncommittally.

Why don't I feel anything? she thought.

"You heard?"

"Yeah."

Yeah, I heard. But I don't care.

"Stan must be taking it hard, Dore."

"I guess he must." Dore ran her hand down her arm and shivered a little. I can feel that, she thought.

When you were dead, you couldn't feel anything at all.

Carol said, "No one saw her leave last night."

Dore felt something then. Relief. "What exactly happened?"

"Don't you know?" Carol waited.

"I just asked."

Carol never could resist a newscast. "She fell down the stairs at school. The ones to the parking lot. That's what they're saying. She told Stan she'd be right back, only she never hit the Girls'. At least, no one saw her in there."

"What was she doing in the back?"

"Some people," Carol lowered her voice, "said she'd been drinking."

"Gwen didn't drink," said Dore, unaccountably irritated.

"She got drunk at that monster party at Megan's."

"And sick like a dog, Carol. Remember?"

"Maybe she thought she just needed practice."

Dore said impatiently, "What if she had been drinking? What difference does it make?"

"That's why she fell!" exclaimed Carol. "Didn't feel a thing. Just went . . ."

"Carol."

"Oh. Right. Dore, I am sorry. Poor Gwen. I mean, I know you and she weren't exactly getting along . . ."

"Really?"

"Well," said Carol. "You know. About you and Stan and all . . ."

"Gwen and I had talked about that. We'd come to an understanding."

Now Carol said, "Really."

"I need to rest, Carol, okay?"

"Yeah. Listen, the funeral's going to be day after tomorrow."

"Thanks," Dore said and hung up.

The procession of cars wound down the narrow road to the cemetery.

Dore sat on the seat next to Carol, careful to keep her face expressionless. Why had she agreed to come to this? Why, why, why?

And why with Carol? Who had said to Dore, "I didn't know what to wear to a funeral. I've never been to one. Do I look all right?"

"Yes," Dore had said through stiff lips.

"You look — you look good," Carol had said, eyeing Dore intently. "Have you ever been to a funeral?"

"No."

What was *wrong* with Carol? Why was she rattling on and on and on?

Carol's just like that, Dore told herself. She likes to talk.

But something wasn't right. Dore felt like an actor in a play, as if Carol were saying all the lines, and Dore wasn't responding correctly.

What did Carol want?

Why did she make Dore feel so afraid?

Carol pulled her car to a stop and they got out. "Everybody's here," she informed Dore. "The whole school."

"You said that," Dore snapped.

"Hey, take it easy, Dore."

Dore turned away and her eyes met Stan's. He was hunched against the sudden sharp wind that seemed to have come up out of nowhere, his hands in the pockets of his coat, looking ill at ease in his suit and tie. He stared at her hard.

Dore looked hastily away. It seemed as if the whole school *was* here.

Everyone except Luci.

Remembering Luci's face when she'd asked her if she was going to Gwen's funeral, Dore pulled her coat around her a little more tightly.

"Dore. Dearest." Luci had stopped. And, incredibly, smiled. "I don't *do* funerals. *That* is not my scene."

"What is?" Dore had snapped.

"Funerals are just bodies," said Luci. "Bodies don't interest me. Except," she amended hastily, "in the — biblical — sense." Then, even more incredibly, she had laughed.

Dore had been outraged. "Stop it!" she cried.

Luci had instantly become solemn again. "I'm

sorry," she'd said. "Tragedy just affects some people that way. It's like, you know, laughing in church, I guess. You don't mean to." Then her expression had been earnest. Sincere.

"I know," said Dore. But when her eyes had met Luci's, she could have sworn, for all of Luci's solemn, sad expression, that little imps of laughter were dancing in Luci's eyes.

"Dore?" Carol touched Dore's elbow. "Come on."

They walked between the polished granite and the marble, past the fading plastic flowers and dying real ones. The ground was spongy and wet, and Dore's heels kept digging in, making it hard for her to keep up.

They gathered at the grave. The casket was a polished thing, a mahogany bullet. Dore looked at it, then quickly looked away.

I won't think about it, she thought.

And thought about Gwen. Remembered. Remembered too much.

"No," she said aloud, oblivious to the looks cast in her direction.

"Dore," hissed Carol.

"Sorry," Dore muttered. "Sorry. I have to . . . I have to get away."

Without waiting for Carol to answer, she turned and walked unsteadily away from the open grave, the closed coffin.

I didn't do it, she told herself. It was an accident. A mistake.

And then a harder, colder voice said, *and she deserved it.*

"No," Dore said again. The word blew away on the cold, cold wind.

And the voice inside going. *Her fault,* the voice insisted. She started it. You are not on this earth to take care of losers. Especially when they double-cross you.

I can't stand this, thought Dore.

Behind her, she heard a creaking sound. She turned. The casket was being lowered into the earth.

She looked wildly around. Row upon row of graves stretched away from her.

"I didn't do it," she said.

But the voice was silent. This time, it didn't answer.

The people began to move. She heard murmurings, sobs. She heard, now, the dull thud of clods of earth being thrown onto the casket.

She had to get away. Far, far away. She started to run, stumbling clumsily. Dodging in and out among the trees, as if something were chasing her.

As if Gwen were behind her.

Until at last, out of breath, she stopped to lean against a twisted little tree.

She was alone.

The funeral was a small disturbance of people dressed in black, pressed against a lowering sky. It wasn't real.

"I won't think about it," she said. "I can't think about it."

She felt a little calmer. A little saner. "I didn't do it," she said. "What happened between me and Gwen, it wasn't my fault. Gwen did it."

Yes. Yes, that sounded right.

She straightened up and began to walk back across the slippery earth to the row of cars that was gradually filling up with people again. Time to go back.

She'd almost reached the cars when something made her look back. A familiar figure was standing at the far edge of the graveyard.

In spite of years of her mother's nonfrown regime, Dore frowned.

Luci?

She blinked.

And the figure was gone.

"Did you see that?" she asked Carol.

Carol's expression changed from one of intense sympathy to one of almost ludicrous curiosity. "See what?"

"I thought I saw . . ." Dore stopped. What was it in Carol's eyes? A sort of greed. A sort of relish.

"A ghost?" prompted Carol.

"A ghost? Why would I see a ghost?"

Carol shrugged unconvincingly. "It *is* a graveyard."

"In the middle of the day," Dore answered brusquely. "Besides, I don't believe in ghosts."

Carol opened the door of the car and slid in. She made a great show of turning the key, fastening her seat belt. But Dore couldn't shake the impression that Carol was somehow watching her. Testing her.

"Sometimes, when people . . . have a lot on their minds . . . they think they see . . . things."

"Well, I'm not seeing things, Carol, okay?" Dore snapped.

Carol adjusted the rearview mirror. She stared into it for a long time.

"What *are* you looking at?" asked Dore.

"Nothing," said Carol, hastily accelerating.

Dore looked back.

Stan was still standing by his car, his hands in the pockets of his coat. He was staring after them intently.

That night Dore sat in her room in the dark. There were shadows in the mirrors on the wall. Shadows on the floor through the windows where the curtains were drawn back. The room was full of shadows.

Dore sat in the deepest shadow of all, her back against the wall. She was staring at the shadows.

She was trying to think of nothing at all.

The phone rang.

Dore forgot. She answered. "Hello?"

"Murderer," the voice whispered.

"Who is this?" she demanded. "Stan! Stan, I know it's you!"

"Murdererrr," said the voice, a voice unlike any she'd ever heard.

"Stan . . ." she almost whimpered.

"Pretty is as pretty dies," the voice said. It was a caress, a loving sigh, a chilling whisper.

She slammed the phone down.

It rang again.

And again.

And again.

At last it stopped.

She sat there in the shadows, staring at it. Who was calling her? Why? What did they know?

And who would they tell?

The shadows in the room deepened. The wind rose. Knobby branches on gnarled trees twisted and danced in arthritic glee.

The shadows in the room didn't dance. They grew longer. Longer. Until they reached across the bed where Dore was sleeping.

When the shadows touched her cheek, she turned her head away and moaned. They moved across her bed, across her body.

She took a deep breath of shadowed air, shuddered, and was still.

It was dark now. Very, very dark. It was a place without light or air.

Dore opened her eyes, but she couldn't see.

She turned over. Her shoulder hit something hard. Her cheek slid across slippery satin.

She tried to sit up.

She couldn't.

She tried to put up her hand, to feel above her. But she couldn't raise her arm. She tried to swing it out to one side and lift it that way.

But her arm hit something hard and solid there, too.

Sudden panic rose in her throat. She flung both hands out — and hit the hard sides of a box.

"No!" she screamed.

She was in a coffin.

Now she kicked, and kicked, pounding, struggling. Her hands grew bloody.

And her panic began to suck all the rest of the air out of the coffin fast. So fast.

No one heard her screaming. No one came to help her at all.

She'd been buried alive.

The shadows slid away from the bed.

Flailing, choking, Dore tore the covers from over her head. She could breathe. She was alive. It had all been a bad dream.

She took deep breaths. They sounded like sobs.

Gradually her heart began to beat normal again.

Just a dream.

Just a nightmare.

She put her hand up to wipe away the tears. Felt the warmth of her skin. The smooth, perfect, living warmth of it.

This is real, she thought. I don't believe in dreams. Or nightmares. Or ghosts.

"Gwen is dead," she said aloud, deliberately. "I didn't do anything wrong. It was all her fault."

Gwen was a loser, thought Dore.

She looked across the shadowed room. The wind was making the shadows dance and dance across the floor.

"Good-bye, Gwen," she said. And fell into a deep and dreamless sleep.

Chapter 15

Smile.

Pose.

Change.

"I love it, doll. Love it, love it, love it."

I bet you do, she thought.

Smile.

Pose.

"Okay. Let's take a break, doll."

She held her pose a moment longer, watching the photographer stare down into his lens, getting his kicks second hand for just a second longer — proof that the sleek gold bathing suit, cut way high on the bottom, and way low on the top, did what it was supposed to do.

Made a splash. Dumb joke, Dore, she told herself. Especially considering this was one bathing suit that was never meant to go near the water . . .

Klaxon was good. The best photographer around. And she needed the best. Everything, *everything* for this audition had to be right.

For one uncomfortable moment she thought of Gwen. Gwen in the dressing room at Rice's, choosing the dress for her first dance. Wanting everything to be perfect. Just perfect . . .

"Head shots next, okay?"

She broke the pose jerkily, picked up her robe, and wrapped it around her. "I'll change back into — something more comfortable."

Klaxon grinned. "Fine by me, doll."

In the dressing room she redid her makeup. Close-ups made different shadows, required different highlights. Without thinking, she pulled out of her purse the mirror Luci had given her and raised it.

A stranger looked back at her. A stranger with her lips, her eyes. But the face was the face of a fiend.

She must have made some sound as she fell back from what she saw. Or maybe it was the sound of her chair crashing over. At any rate, Klaxon's face appeared around the edge of the door.

"What'sa matter, doll?"

She was shaking. Could he tell? He *must not* know. He mustn't, *must not* see that mirror.

"Nothing." She laid the mirror face down on the dressing table. Carefully. "Must be getting tired. I'll be right out."

But Klaxon had already come into the dressing room, righting the chair, leaning over to pick up the mirror.

Don't, she almost whimpered.

"Pretty," said Klaxon, examining the scene chased in silver across the back. He turned it over thoughtfully, then held it up and studied his reflection in it. "Nice old mirror," he said indifferently. "Make a nice prop . . . nice true image, too. Doesn't have the usual warp in the glass that you see in some of these old jobs."

"W-what do you mean?"

"You know — distortion. Back when they made this mirror, they were probably still in the Dark Ages when it came to grinding and polishing lenses. That's really what a mirror is, you know. . . ."

Putting the mirror down, he lounged back toward the door. "C'mon," he said. "We're gettin' some good shots. Don't wanna lose the edge."

"Coming." She looked down at the mirror. *I'm working too hard,* she told herself.

"Doll." Klaxon's voice sounded faintly irritable. With an act of will she took the mirror and shoved it into her tote bag. Klaxon didn't shoot just anyone. Having Klaxon's name on your portfolio meant you had potential. He had the eye.

And it was Klaxon's eye that counted. Not some mirror's. Stupid mirror.

She heard the soft word, breathed into the phone. *Murderer.*

No. She wasn't.

But maybe someone thought she was. Someone like Stan.

Stan. What a freak he was. And what a stunt-man.

Stan could rig a mirror to drive her crazy. To pay her back.

After all, hadn't he tried to kill her once before?

She was shaking again. She had to stop.

Or she might lose everything she had worked so hard to get.

"Spill," said Luci. Dore had picked up the contact sheets after school. Now she and Luci were sitting in Dore's room, Luci on the floor, her back pressed against the mirror, Dore facing Luci, also on the floor, on her stomach. The envelope with the contact sheets lay between them.

"This is old stuff for you, right?" Luci went on.

"Not with Klaxon. I was surprised he took me. My mother tried to get him to shoot me once before. He told her he wasn't into beauty queens."

Luci smiled. "Clearly you are now becoming more than a beauty queen . . . oh, wow!" Catching one of the contact sheets between her fingertips, she held it up, tilting her head to one side to study it. Her long red hair fell over one shoulder, picking up the late afternoon light with a fiery answering shimmer. Today she was wearing a pale green silk top that wrapped seductively around her, caught at the hip in a knot above a short, almond-colored skirt. Her legs, tucked under her like a cat's, looked impossibly long.

Looking at Luci, seeing her own reflection over Luci's shoulder, Dore felt, for just a moment, as if the room had rocked slightly. Neither of them, somehow, looked real.

Stop it, she told herself.

No way, said a little voice inside her head. Play and pay.

"*Niiiice*," said Luci.

"Wh-hat?"

"You take a decent picture."

"K-Klaxon," Dore managed to get out. She took the contact sheet back with nerveless fingers and carefully slid it back into the envelope.

"No," said Luci. "He had to have someone to work with. No false modesty, Dore. Who's gonna look out for you except you, right?"

Dore answered automatically, without thinking. "My parents."

Luci shook her head. "As long as you're their good little girl. As long as you do what they say . . . but the moment you try to have your own life, they'll be all over you."

"Maybe."

"If you don't believe me, why haven't you told your parents about the audition?"

"I will, I will."

"Afterwards. Am I right?"

"Do you always have to be right?" Dore was irritated now, not only by Luci's casual assumption of superiority, but by how very accurately she had caught on to Dore's reasoning. Dore hadn't told her parents because she knew her mother would disapprove. Oh, her mother was the original Beauty Queen's Maniac Mother, true. But both her father and her mother had never deviated from their plans for Dore. College, college, always college. And not just any college. The right college. Every pageant won had meant, among other things, more money in the college fund.

But come to think of it, why had they made her put all her money away in a college fund? It wasn't as if her parents didn't have plenty of money.

"Hey, I didn't mean to burn you. . . ."

Dore came back to the conversation with a jolt. "No, no problem."

But she couldn't help thinking: What had her parents done with all that money?

Chapter 16

"So, Mother."

"Yes, dear?" Mrs. Grey poured the coffee herself. It was Sunday and Mrs. Bauer's day off, and Mrs. Grey had spent the better part of the morning making an exquisite breakfast of fresh fruit and warmed-up croissants. It did look charming on the table in the garden, against the checkered café tablecloth.

"You know all those prizes I won in pageants?"

"Umm." Mrs. Grey smiled benignly at the garden. Her husband might read all those horticultural magazines, but she, clearly, was the one with the magic touch. Such a lovely garden . . .

"Fruit, dear?"

Dore took an apple. "Mother?"

"Yes? Oh, yes, dear. Yes, you have quite a nice nest egg, dear."

"Why?"

"For college," Mr. Grey said, emerging briefly

115

from behind the gardening section of the Sunday paper.

"Why?"

Her father frowned. "For college."

"No — why did I have to save all that money? Don't we have enough money for me for college?"

"Well, of course, dear. But it's nice to have a little extra." Her mother was looking distressed.

"Why couldn't I have had the money? To spend when I wanted?"

"But, dear, why would you want it? Don't we give you everything you need?"

"So . . ." Dore put the half-eaten apple down on her plate. "All that time I could have had money of my own. But you kept it."

"We didn't keep it," said her father impatiently. "We put it in long-term accounts for you. Your college is paid for, and you'll have a little extra to get started or go further in school afterwards."

"Suppose I don't want to go to school? Suppose I wanted to . . . to move to New York and become an actor?"

"Nonsense." Her father went back to the paper.

Dore turned to her mother. "Suppose I wanted my money? Suppose I wanted it now?"

"But why?" said her mother. She looked around, as if the answer might be hanging from one of the trees.

"Because it's mine."

"But darling . . ."

"Can I have it?"

"Oh, dear. You know, Dore, we only want to do what's best for — "

"Can I have my money?"

"No." Her father didn't even bother to look up from his newspaper.

"Why not? It's *mine*."

"Your father's right, Dore, darling. You'll be glad when you get to college."

"I want my money," said Dore.

"That's enough," her father growled.

"It's *my* money."

Her father put his paper down with ominous calm.

"Dore," her mother interposed hastily. "You're not feeling yourself. Gwen's death . . . you're upset."

Dore took a deep breath. "What has that got to do with what you did with my money?"

Her mother tried again. "Is there something in particular you want to buy? Because I'm sure we could work it out."

"I want my money. *My money*."

"You may leave the table, Dore." Her father was very angry. Frighteningly so. But Dore wasn't afraid of him anymore.

"Don't think you can get away with this," said Dore.

"Dore!" cried her mother.

Rising from the table, Dore looked contemptuously at her parents. They'd be sorry. Very sorry.

She'd show them.

"You're thieves," said Dore.

Her father stood up so suddenly, Dore's mother gave a squeak of alarm.

Dore smiled.

"You're thieves," she repeated. "And you'll be sorry."

Ignoring her mother's heartbroken cry, she turned and left the garden.

That night she lay in her bed, drowsily watching the lights reflected by the mirrors onto her walls and ceilings. Sort of like the spotlights you saw on television at the openings. Or at the Academy Awards.

Someday she'd be there. The applause would pour down on her like gold. And, oh, how they'd hate her as they applauded. She was no fool. Nobody really loved a winner. But as long as you were the winner, it didn't matter.

And she wasn't going to thank her parents. She wasn't going to thank anybody but herself.

Tomorrow was the audition. Tomorrow was the beginning.

Her secret. She hadn't even told Corbin. Only Luci knew. For a moment that thought bothered Dore. Then she remembered that Luci wasn't even trying out, although she'd offered to drive Dore to the audition.

But Dore wasn't about to fall for that Miss Congeniality routine. She was taking her mother's car. Early. She'd leave a note and by the time she got back, all her mother's recriminations and her father's pathetic attempts at punishment wouldn't matter.

Because she'd be packing to leave.

Tomorrow, thought Dore, is the first day of the rest of my life.

It was a bright and sunny day.

Dore had eased the Seville down the driveway shortly after dawn. An easy drive, made easier by the plans she was making. She barely noticed where she was going until she got there — with plenty of time to spare.

Using her mother's credit card, she got a room at a hotel near where the auditions were being held. A good room. Soaking and splashing in the jacuzzi, she congratulated herself on her forethought. This was much, much better than sneaking around in the dark in her room, trying to get ready.

When she finished dressing, she stepped back to survey the results.

She'd never looked so good.

Never.

Unearthly good, she thought. Wicked good.

She smiled at herself in the mirror.

Then she remembered Luci's mirror. Some impulse had made her tuck it into her tote. Some impulse now made her reach into the bag and draw it out.

At arm's length, mirror side down, she examined it. Just a mirror. A heavy, weird old mirror. An antique. A fossil.

It felt strangely warm in her hand, and heavier. She turned it over and watched a glint of light it caught play on the wall.

"Just a mirror," she said aloud and raised it resolutely to eye level.

A monster was looking back at her — a creature so hideous that Dore couldn't look away. Transfixed, she stared at the ruined face: Sagging scars of flesh and strips of wattled, mottled skin hung on a skull that seemed about to pierce through the veins that lashed the whole together. In sunken pouches the lashless eyes looked out, meeting hers.

Dore gasped for air.

The lipless mouth opened, taking its own evil breath. Foul, uneven teeth showed beneath it, and a bulbous tongue flickered out like a snake's and ran across where the lips should have been.

"This is me!" thought Dore wildly.

This can't be me.

She dropped the mirror and, without looking to see where it fell, turned blindly toward the door. Clutching her tote, she groped her way out into the hall.

"Are you all right, miss?" said the elevator man.

She nodded dumbly. "Some fresh air," she gasped.

The doors of the elevator opened, and she stumbled across the lobby. She caught a glimpse of herself in the huge mirrors flanking the entrance.

She flinched. Then stopped.

It was only herself looking back. In the lobby

mirrors, she could see that others were looking, too — at her. And there was nothing but frank appreciation in their eyes.

I am beautiful, she thought.

I am.

Stupid nerves.

Stupid mirror.

Straightening her shoulders, she swept out of the lobby and into the street.

She had four blocks to walk, and plenty of time. Putting on her dark glasses, she strolled along. Soon she wouldn't be able to walk anonymously on any street. Soon she would be walking on the best streets in the best cities in the world. Soon she'd have money, fame, everything.

Soon, she'd make anybody who ever crossed her sorry. Very sorry.

That was power. Absolute power.

Suddenly she caught a glimpse of flaming red ahead of her.

Dore's steps quickened.

A sleek, lithe figure in a narrow black outfit strode ahead of her. Dore would have known that walk anywhere.

It was Luci.

That sneak. That liar.

Luci was here to try to ruin her chances. No way, Luci.

"No way," Dore said aloud.

She picked up the pace. They were almost there. Luci walked along so gracefully, so seductively, as if she owned the whole world.

It wasn't fair.

Ahead, a DON'T WALK sign began to flash. Luci slowed to a stop.

The traffic hummed along. The sunlight was blinding. Impervious to the passersby she shouldered out of the way, Dore hurried on, intent only on one thing.

Luci.

Luci.

Good-bye, Luci.

She lunged for Luci. She threw her whole weight into the push. A hundred thousand workouts had made her body perfect. And strong.

Luci was going to die.

Good-bye, Luci.

Someone shrieked.

She heard horns, the screaming of brakes.

And, then, somehow, she had slipped past Luci and was plunging out, like a diver off the high dive, head first into the street.

For one moment she struggled, half on her knees, as if by lunging a little further she might be safe. For one moment she forgot who she was and where she was and thought only of that safe place just beyond her outstretched, grasping hands.

If only she could . . .

Then the car hit her and rolled over her and began to drag her along.

She never had a chance.

And then she was gone.

Chapter 17

She woke up in a room made of shadows.

A white room, with white shadows going in and out. She couldn't see them clearly. Everything swam away from her when she tried to see.

Soon she gave up trying, and let the shadows get darker and darker until she went back down into darkness.

Then she heard one of the shadows whispering to her.

"Dore? Darling?"

"She can't hear you," another familiar-sounding shadow said.

"It is unlikely," said a third shadow, an official sounding one.

She tried to say that she could hear. But the effort made everything swim away again, and the darkness descended.

Then, gradually, the shadows became more distinct. Men and women in crisp white uniforms. White walls and white blinds that were always closed, white, antiseptic smelling sheets, and cold metal and the prick of things in her arms at various intervals.

And then one day the shadow that was her mother swam into clear focus and said, "Dore, darling? Do you know where you are?"

And Dore, painfully forcing her lips apart, answered, "A hospital."

Several shadows came in and out at once, although Dore now knew they were nurses. Her mother was crying. Why was her mother crying?

Her mother wasn't the one in the hospital.

"Why?" Dore croaked.

"Shhh, darling," said her mother, and there was another needle prick and darkness.

In between the darkness and the shadows, there was pain. It had a sort of silver color behind her eyelids. She would drift into consciousness on the sensation of movement and realize that she was being wheeled somewhere on a hospital trolley. Then there would be spotlights, and hands and instruments touching her.

Mostly touching her face.

She tried to pull away once.

The needle came back and pricked her. She just had time to hear someone say, quite clearly, "Poor kid," before she went out again.

Finally, she woke up and said, "What happened?" — and no one said, "Shhh."

Her mother said, "Oh, Dore."

With an effort, Dore turned her face toward the

foot of the bed where her father was standing.

"You were in an accident," her father said. "You fell in front of a car. You are at Mercy General. You've been here for quite some time."

Dore tried to frown, and nails of pain drove into her skull.

Something about the wrinkle squad . . .

"Don't you remember?" her mother whispered. "You'd taken the car. You left a note. Something about an audition for a movie . . ."

"Audition?"

"It didn't make any sense. No audition of any sort, here or anywhere nearby," said her father crisply.

Then it came back to her. "I missed it. No!" She tried to sit up. Her mother clutched her arm and tried to press her back down.

"No," croaked Dore. "No, no, no . . ."

Then the nurse was there, and although Dore tried to roll away, tried to fight free, tried to make them see how important it was for her to get up and get out of that stupid hospital, it didn't help.

The darkness won again.

She had an armful of flowers, like they always gave you at the pageants. People were lined up on either side of her, applauding her as she walked by.

But it was all wrong.

She looked down as she ran and saw that the roses were full of thorns. No, not thorns. Hooks. Horrible silver hooks like fishhooks.

They were tearing her dress, hooking into her flesh.

She tried to fling the flowers away, but they clung to her.

Ahead was the end of the runway.

She stumbled toward it, trying to strip the flowers away.

Someone was there, waiting for her.

It was Luci. "You won," said Luci and shoved Dore off the end of the runway.

Then there was blood everywhere.

She reached up to her face and pulled her hands back covered with blood. Blood and rose petals.

The smell was sickening.

Dore twisted awake. It was dark. The hospital was still.

Lying there, Dore remembered.

She remembered everything.

The blinds went up with a snap.

"Darling," her mother said anxiously. "Keep in mind how well you've done. Splendidly. And, of course, we've only just begun."

"Precisely," said the doctor. He finished peeling back the last bit of gauze.

Mr. Grey cleared his throat and looked away.

The doctor said, "Consider that you are lucky. Between the glass and the metal, you could have suffered extensive permanent brain injuries. Lost your vision. Even your life.

"The damage, therefore, to your face, is, relatively speaking, remarkably superficial."

"Let me see," said Dore.

"Dear."

"I said, Mother, let me see."

The doctor reached over to the bedside table and handed Dore a mirror just as Dore's mother picked up another mirror from the dresser by the bed.

The mirror the doctor handed Dore was plastic, and light, and cool.

And accurate. Dore held it up.

Her face would have sunk a thousand ships. Broken a camera to bits. Made a dog howl. A child scream in terror.

It was puckered and twisted with scars. Hideous. A monster was looking back at her.

"Just the beginning," her mother began again. "There are specialists . . ."

"I want to be alone," said Dore.

"But . . ."

"Give her some time," said the doctor. He stood up, frowning. Not quite looking at her face.

Her mother began to cry. Her father put his arm around her mother's shoulders and led her out of the room.

Still holding a mirror in each hand, Dore closed her eyes.

She didn't know how much time had passed before she sensed someone at the door. She looked, half expecting to see Luci.

But it was Stan . . .

Stan's eyes widened as Dore turned full face toward him.

"What's the matter?" said Dore. "Haven't you ever seen a monster before?"

"Dore . . ."

"I can't have visitors," said Dore.

"You can't?"

"No. Go away. Go gloat somewhere else. Go tell the world you've seen a monster."

"Dore. God, Dore, I'm sorry. . . ."

"Big deal. Go away."

But Stan came closer, staring, mesmerized. "Dore."

She closed her eyes so she wouldn't have to watch him watch her. "What?"

"I had to . . . I had to tell you. It was Gwen."

"Gwen's dead," said Dore dully.

"Gwen hid at the school that time. She pushed you. She even borrowed some of my tiger props to scare you. I didn't even know about it until that night you told her I'd done it. She didn't mean anything by it. It was just a — a warning."

Dore said, "And then you called me up and said I was a murderer?"

"Yeah, yeah, I did. I couldn't believe Gwen was dead. I blamed you. I'm sorry, Dore."

"Don't be."

The room was silent. Finally, Stan said, "I guess I'll go now."

"Good-bye," said Dore.

But when he reached the door, she said, "Wait a minute."

Stan turned. But only enough to see her out of the corner of his eye.

"Stan . . . where's Luci?"

"Luci?"

"Luci. Yeah, where is she?"

"She's gone. Like the same day you — this happened. Transferred, they said. She told Carol she was going to where it was always warm . . . didn't she tell you?"

Dore smiled.

Stan gasped.

Dore could imagine what her scarred, twisted, gap-toothed smile looked like. "Boo," she said.

Stan gulped, and hurried out of the room.

It was a room without mirrors.

Except for two.

Carefully, Dore laid the plastic mirror on the bedside table.

Then she raised the heavy silver mirror up to eye level.

The monster was gone.

The most beautiful girl in the world was looking back at her.

She had skin as white as snow, lips as red as cherries. Her eyes were as blue as a summer day, and her hair shone like the sun. She was a princess in a fairy tale.

"Mirror, mirror, on the wall, who's the fairest of them all?" said Dore.

And she began to laugh.

She laughed and laughed.

Somewhere, dimly, she heard the beepers go off. They'd be coming with the needles again soon.

But she kept laughing.

She laughed until the tears ran down her face.

And the fairest of them all, who was gone forever now, laughed back from the mirror with her.

A Sneak Preview of
R.L. STINE'S
latest superthriller,

BEACH
HOUSE

3
Worried About Sharks

"Did you have a good time with Stuart?" Amy asked.

Maria nodded, smiling coyly.

"The movie was really neat," Amy said.

"Our speaker wasn't working too well," Maria said. "We had to move the car to three different spots before we found a good one."

It was the following afternoon, a bright but overcast day, hazy with a fog moving in off the ocean. The two friends had decided to take a long walk along the shore since the sun wasn't cooperating.

"Did Stuart take his dad's Thunderbird?" Amy asked. She had been pumping Maria all afternoon for details about the night before, but with little success. Maria was in one of her quieter, more thoughtful moods.

"Yeah," she replied, staring into the white haze

over the water. "It's a real dreamy car. Like something in a magazine."

"I think Stuart really digs you," Amy said, turning her eyes to Maria's.

"Well . . . I guess I dig him, too," Maria replied after a long while. "He's a little immature, but — "

" — All boys are immature," Amy interrupted. She bent down to pick up a clamshell.

Maria gazed straight ahead at the mysterious beach house a few hundred yards in front of them. The white, hazy afternoon light made the house seem even darker than usual. The tide was coming in, and waves rushed under the house, frothing white against the stilts, then pulling back with a *whoosh*.

Suddenly, as she stared, the glass door facing the ocean slid open, and a figure came running out, running at full speed toward them. As if he had spotted them from inside the house.

"Buddy!"

Maria's stomach knotted in dread.

She hadn't looked forward to seeing him, to having to explain why she had stood him up the night before.

She knew he'd be angry. About that. And about the swim trunks.

He hated to be teased. And yesterday was much worse than teasing.

"Hey — " he called to them, waving as he ran.

Maybe I should turn and run, Maria thought in

a panic. She glanced at Amy and caught a fearful expression on her face as well.

But there was nowhere to run.

Besides, that would be childish.

She had just been talking about how childish and immature boys were. She had to face him like a mature adult.

"Hi, how's it going?" he asked, his bare feet skidding to a stop a few yards in front of them. He smiled, first at Amy, then at Maria, his eyes lingering on Maria.

He was wearing a sleeveless, blue cotton T-shirt and baggy Hawaiian-style swim trunks. He had a white beach towel wrapped around his broad shoulders, which were already tanned, even though summer had just begun.

"Hi." Maria gave him a shy wave. "About last night — "

"The sun should burn through soon," he said, shielding his eyes with one hand and peering up at the bright white sky. "Have you been in the water?"

"No. Brrrrr," Amy replied, wrapping her hands around her shoulders, pretending to shiver.

"No. The water's really warm," Buddy said, gripping the ends of the towel around his neck with both hands. "I guess because the air is cold."

Maria waited for him to return his eyes to her.

Was he avoiding her?

Was he so angry at her that he planned to ignore her?

No.

He reached out and swatted a green fly off her shoulder. "Look out. The green ones bite."

"They sprayed the beach and the dunes with DDT last week," Amy said.

"But it only kills the mosquitoes. Not the flies," Buddy told her.

"About last night," Maria said, practically bursting to make her phony excuse. "I'm really sorry, Buddy."

His brown eyes narrowed, but his easy, relaxed expression remained. "Hey, I thought we were going to go into town and mess around," he said casually.

"Yeah. I know." Maria glanced at Amy, who turned her eyes to the ocean. "I wanted to. But I wasn't feeling very well. Too much sun."

She studied his face, trying to determine if he was believing her at all. If only I were a better liar, she thought. Maria could hear her voice trembling guiltily, and she knew that she was blushing. "I tried to call you — " she started to add.

"There's no phone in the beach house," he interrupted, gesturing back to the shadowy structure perched over the shore.

"No phone?" Amy asked, feeling it was safe to return to the conversation.

"The phone lines don't go that far. The house is out of the town's limits or something." He turned back to Maria, his face filled with concern. "Are you feeling better?"

She nodded, feeling even more guilty. "Yeah. I'm really sorry about last night."

"Hey. No big deal," he said, shrugging. "I'm just glad you're feeling okay."

Maria stared at him, studying his dark features, surprised by his casual reaction to being stood up.

I guess he believes me, she thought.

Maybe I'm not such a bad liar after all.

"Sorry about yesterday," Amy said. "You know. The swim trunks and everything." Her gray-blue eyes twinkled, and she was unable to keep a mischievous grin from spreading across her pale face.

"Amy and I tried to get your trunks away from the boys," Maria said quickly. "How did you get back?"

"I swam," Buddy said, frowning.

Maria thought she detected a flash of anger in his eyes, but it quickly faded.

"I swam to my house," he said, gesturing with his head to the beach house. "Then I just ran inside. No big deal."

"But that was a long swim," Amy insisted. "We were way down there, by the lifeguard station." She pointed.

"Luckily the current was going my way," Buddy explained, tugging the towel behind his neck first one way, then the other. "I sort of floated most of the way, just let it carry me."

"That was a dumb joke," Maria said, shaking her head, then nervously tugging at her black ponytail. "Sometimes Ronnie and Stuart — "

"I was pretty cold when I finally got out," Buddy admitted. "But, hey — I'll pay them back." He laughed. Mirthless laughter. Not as casual as he had intended.

Amy tossed the clamshell into the water.

"How about a swim?" Buddy asked suddenly, tossing the towel to the sand.

"It's awfully cold without the sun," Maria said, glancing up at the white glare of the sky.

"It's pretty foggy out there," Amy said.

"The water's real warm, and the waves are gentle," Buddy replied. "Come on. I'll show you."

"I can't," Amy said, glancing at Maria. "I promised I'd take care of my little sister. I'm late already."

"I'll come with you," Maria said quickly.

"No. Stay. Come on. We'll have last night's date today," Buddy urged, grabbing Maria's arm gently.

"Well . . ."

"Yeah. Stay," Amy urged, starting down the beach. "I'm really gonna catch it if I don't hurry. Call you later, Maria." With a wave to them both, she began running across the beach, the man's shirt that she wore over her bathing suit flapping behind her like Superman's cape.

Maria watched Amy until she appeared to be swallowed up by the encroaching fog. Then she turned to Buddy, who was still holding her arm. "You sure you want to swim?"

He nodded, staring into her eyes. "Yeah. Come on. It'll be great. Just the two of us." His expression remained earnest, but his dark eyes suddenly seemed alive, excited.

"I'm not that good a swimmer," Maria admitted, following him as he jogged to the water's edge.

"Look how calm it is," he said, pointing.

The waves were low, lapping softly against the sand before sliding back with a gentle *whoosh*.

"Amazing!" Maria exclaimed softly. "It almost looks like a lake." She took a few steps into the water, the water rolling over her ankles, her feet sinking into the sand as she walked. "Ooh — I thought you said it was *warm!*"

Buddy laughed. He was several steps ahead of her, in up to his knees. "You'll get used to it." He came back quickly, taking both of her hands and pulling her out deeper.

"Oh!" Maria cried out from the shock of the cold.

She pulled her hands from his and dived under the water. The only way to get used to it is to get in fast, she thought. Surfacing, she looked for him. He had been right ahead of her. Where had he disappeared to?

"Right here!" he called from behind.

She spun around in the water, disoriented.

There was more of an undertow than she had thought.

"I got turned around," she explained, swimming to him.

"Let's go out further and get away from the undertow," he said. He ducked under the water, then surfaced, taking long, steady strokes, gliding easily.

He's a really good swimmer, Maria thought. She found herself to be a little surprised. He had always seemed so awkward, almost clumsy, on shore.

She did pretty well in the water, considering she'd only had a few months of Red Cross lessons at the Y, and never really got to swim except during her family vacations in Dunehampton. She was probably a better swimmer than she'd realized. She just didn't have much confidence.

"Hey — we're getting pretty far from shore!" she called to Buddy.

But he didn't react, didn't seem to hear her. He was several yards ahead of her now, swimming straight and fast despite the roll and sway of the water.

"Hey — Buddy!" Maria called.

He kept swimming, his arms stretching out in those long, regular strokes, his face turned away from her.

"Buddy!"

Her arms ached. She floated for a moment, catching her breath.

"Buddy — too far!"

The fog seemed to swirl about her. She turned back. The shore was a faint outline, buried in haze . . . so far away.

The dark water offered the only color out here. Everything else was gray and white, the white glare of the sky, the gray fog . . . circling her, circling her.

"Buddy!" she screamed.

Where was he?

Was she all alone out here?

All alone in the fog?

The water rolled and tilted, tossing her one way, then another.

I'm dizzy, she thought.

And then she scolded herself: Don't panic.

You're a good swimmer. And you're not really that far from shore.

The fog just makes it seem farther.

The white glare and the fog.

She closed her eyes for a moment, swimming hard.

"Buddy!"

And there he was. At her side.

"What's wrong?" He flashed her a reassuring smile. He wasn't even out of breath.

"I — didn't see you." She held onto his shoulder, surprisingly muscular. He had never seemed very strong on shore.

"Here I am." She had never seen him smile so broadly, so easily. He seemed so *happy* out here.

But she was frightened now. Of the fog. Of how far they'd swum.

"I want to go back, Buddy."

He lowered his lips in a pout, playful but seriously disappointed. "Just a little farther. The water's so great today."

She realized she was still gripping his shoulder. "I'm cold. And I'm worried."

His eyes widened.

They both bobbed as a current carried them to the side. It felt cold, colder than the water that remained behind it.

"We're not that far," he said, gazing back to shore.

"There were sharks. Remember? Not too far out," she said.

"Sharks won't bother you," he said, his expression a blank, his dark eyes suddenly dull. "Unless they smell blood."

Was he trying to scare her? To be funny?

Why did he say that?

"No. Really," she said, and then sputtered as she swallowed a mouthful of water.

When she stopped choking, trying to spit out the salty taste, he was swimming again, pulling himself further out, deeper into the swirling, heavy grayness of the low fog.

"No — Buddy — wait!"

He stopped his stroke, floated, waited for her to catch up.

"Buddy — really. I want to go back now. I'm not that good a swimmer."

To her surprise, his expression had completely changed. It was as if all the warmth had floated away. He stared at her with cold, narrowed eyes.

He grabbed her shoulder. Hard.

"I'm going to take care of you," he said. Without warmth or concern.

"What?" Was he trying to reassure her? That didn't seem to be his intention.

4
Hurt Feelings

"Let go!" Maria repeated.

Buddy released his grip and gave her a hard shove.

She felt suddenly heavy, heavy with fear. So heavy, she felt that she might sink, just drop out of sight to the bottom of the ocean and never come up.

Why was he glaring at her like that?

What had she *done*?

"You hurt my feelings," he said, as if answering her question.

A strong current raised them both up toward the graying sky, swirled them around. Thick wisps of fog lowered around them, floating toward the shore.

I'm dreaming, Maria thought. This is a bad dream.

I can't be out in the ocean in the hazy fog, so far

Was he trying to *scare* her? Why would he do that?

"Buddy — I'm going back now."

"No. You're not. I'm going to take care of you, Maria."

Reading his expression, she gasped. "Let go of me!"

from shore, with this boy so filled with anger, with hatred.

"Buddy — it was a joke!" she shouted, pleading, her fear choking the sound of her voice. Again, she swallowed a mouthful of water, salty and thick. She coughed, cleared her throat. "We were just joking!"

"It was no joke!" he screamed, anger tightening his features. *"You hurt my feelings."*

"Well, I'm sorry," she said, turning her eyes to shore. The beach had been swallowed up by the haze. She couldn't tell where the water ended and the land began.

How far out *am* I? she wondered.

Can I make it back by myself?

She realized she was trembling. From the cold? From her fear?

Buddy turned away from her sharply and, with long, steady strokes, swam further out, gliding through the bobbing water.

"No. Buddy — come back!" Maria pleaded. "Please!"

Should she swim after him?

Should she turn toward shore? Try to get back without his help?

She stared through the fog. If only she could see how far from shore she had swum.

If only she weren't so frightened.

He had seemed like such a nice guy. Quiet. Serious.

"Hey!"

He popped up beside her, shouting in her ear.

Startled, she uttered a short cry. "You scared me."

"I know."

"Buddy — stop. You're really scaring me. I want to go back now."

"I know."

"You're not funny," she said, trying to hold herself together, trying to hold back the loud sobs that were welling in her chest, trying to keep the tears from bursting from her eyes.

"I know."

"Stop saying that!" she screamed. "Come on — I'm cold, and I'm frightened."

"I know."

He stared at her, unblinking, silently treading water, his breathing steady, calm.

He's crazy, she thought.

She dived under a sloping wave, turned, and came up facing the shore.

At least she *thought* she was facing the shore. The fog had thickened, had formed a wall between her and the beach.

I don't even know which way to swim, she realized, feeling so heavy now, her arms so heavy, her legs. She had to force herself to keep breathing.

The sky, the gray, hazy sky, seemed low enough to reach up and touch. The wall of fog circled, closed in.

Everything was closing in on her.

Her own heart seemed to close in, to tighten.

"Buddy — what are you going to do? My arms are tired. I can't keep floating like this."

"You hurt my feelings," he repeated, staring hard into her eyes. For the first time, she noticed a slender scar on his chin, like a tiny, white snake catching the white glare of the sky.

"Buddy — can we go back and dry off and talk about it on the beach?" she begged, her voice high and tight, a voice she'd never heard before.

He ignored her question. "You lied to me, Maria."

"Huh?"

I can't breathe, she thought.

I can't breathe, and I can't move my arms.

"I know you went out with Stuart last night."

"I'm sorry, Buddy. Really. I am. But you have to take me back now. *You have to take me back!*"

"I just hate to be lied to," he said flatly, his face expressionless.

Maria suddenly realized he wasn't staring at her. His gaze was over her shoulder, past her in the rolling waters. She turned to see what had caught his eye.

Dark shapes. Skimming rapidly along the surface of the water.

Like submarines. Dark triangles moving silently toward them.

Buddy returned his eyes to hers.

She saw the smile form on his face. The strangest smile.

"Sharks," he said.

point® **THRILLERS**

R.L. Stine

- ☐ MC44236-8 The Baby-sitter — $3.50
- ☐ MC44332-1 The Baby-sitter II — $3.50
- ☐ MC45386-6 Beach House — $3.25
- ☐ MC43278-8 Beach Party — $3.50
- ☐ MC43125-0 Blind Date — $3.50
- ☐ MC43279-6 The Boyfriend — $3.50
- ☐ MC44333-X The Girlfriend — $3.50
- ☐ MC45385-8 Hit and Run — $3.25
- ☐ MC46100-1 The Hitchhiker — $3.50
- ☐ MC43280-X The Snowman — $3.50
- ☐ MC43139-0 Twisted — $3.50

Caroline B. Cooney

- ☐ MC44316-X The Cheerleader — $3.25
- ☐ MC41641-3 The Fire — $3.25
- ☐ MC43806-9 The Fog — $3.25
- ☐ MC45681-4 Freeze Tag — $3.25
- ☐ MC45402-1 The Perfume — $3.25
- ☐ MC44884-6 The Return of the Vampire — $2.95
- ☐ MC41640-5 The Snow — $3.25
- ☐ MC45682-2 The Vampire's Promise — $3.50

Diane Hoh

- ☐ MC44330-5 The Accident — $3.25
- ☐ MC45401-3 The Fever — $3.25
- ☐ MC43050-5 Funhouse — $3.25
- ☐ MC44904-4 The Invitation — $3.50
- ☐ MC45640-7 The Train (9/92) — $3.25

Sinclair Smith

- ☐ MC45063-8 The Waitress — $2.95

Christopher Pike

- ☐ MC43014-9 Slumber Party — $3.50
- ☐ MC44256-2 Weekend — $3.50

A. Bates

- ☐ MC45829-9 The Dead Game — $3.25
- ☐ MC43291-5 Final Exam — $3.25
- ☐ MC44582-0 Mother's Helper — $3.50
- ☐ MC44238-4 Party Line — $3.25

D.E. Athkins

- ☐ MC45246-0 Mirror, Mirror — $3.25
- ☐ MC45349-1 The Ripper — $3.25
- ☐ MC44941-9 Sister Dearest — $2.95

Carol Ellis

- ☐ MC44768-8 My Secret Admirer — $3.25
- ☐ MC46044-7 The Stepdaughter — $3.25
- ☐ MC44916-8 The Window — $2.95

Richie Tankersley Cusick

- ☐ MC43115-3 April Fools — $3.25
- ☐ MC43203-6 The Lifeguard — $3.25
- ☐ MC43114-5 Teacher's Pet — $3.25
- ☐ MC44235-X Trick or Treat — $3.25

Lael Littke

- ☐ MC44237-6 Prom Dress — $3.25

Edited by T. Pines

- ☐ MC45256-8 Thirteen — $3.50

Available wherever you buy books, or use this order form.

point®

Other books you will enjoy, about real kids like you!